A SMOKY MOUNTAIN CHRISTMAS

Gill Robinson's fiancé has called off their Christmas Eve wedding, and she's dreading the upcoming holidays. Out of the blue, she has the chance to escape: her Aunt Betsy has a small B&B in the Smoky Mountains and needs a break, so Gill flies out to help. But when she meets handsome, enigmatic Luke Sawyer, she knows the quiet time she'd envisioned isn't going to happen. Ostensibly the inn's handyman, Gill suspects there's a lot more to Luke than he's letting on . . .

ANGELA BRITNELL

A SMOKY MOUNTAIN CHRISTMAS

Complete and Unabridged

LINFORD
Leicester

First published in Great Britain in 2014

First Linford Edition
published 2016

A catalogue record for this book is available
from the British Library.

ISBN 978–1–4448–2911–2

Published by
F. A. Thorpe (Publishing)
Anstey, Leicestershire

Set by Words & Graphics Ltd.
Anstey, Leicestershire
Printed and bound in Great Britain by
T. J. International Ltd., Padstow, Cornwall

This book is printed on acid-free paper

1

'In case you'd forgotten, I'm a history teacher. I don't know anything about running a bed-and-breakfast,' Gill protested. 'I've never even been to Tennessee. You and Aunt Betsy are both mad, and for another thing . . . '

Patricia Robinson briskly dismissed her only daughter's protests. 'Gillian Elizabeth, stop fussing. You're a perfectly capable young woman. The inn only has four bedrooms, and anyone can fry a bit of bacon. It's only for a fortnight, after all. You told me last week you needed something to . . . occupy yourself over the Christmas holidays.'

'Instead of getting married, you mean?' Gill retorted. She was tired of everyone tiptoeing around the subject of her broken engagement. Three months previously, the man she'd adored since she was sixteen had told her he couldn't go through with their planned Christmas Eve wedding. Apparently he'd fallen in love with the new French teacher at the school where they both worked, and this was 'the real thing'. As opposed to what, she didn't like to ask.

Her mother shook her head sadly. 'You sound so bitter.'

'Are you surprised?' Gill wasn't sure how a woman was supposed to react in these circumstances, but didn't consider her reaction extreme.

'I suppose not.' Patricia shrugged. 'But that's why this will be perfect for you.'

Gill hadn't seen her aunt since Betsy's last visit to Cornwall about eight years ago. Her mother's elder sister had been swept off her feet decades ago by an American stationed at the nearby US Air Force base and whisked away to travel all over the world with him. On his retirement they bought a neglected historic inn on the edge of the Smoky Mountains National Park and renovated it. Unfortunately,

Uncle Hank had died last year, and her aunt was now trying to manage the place on her own. Her health hadn't been good, and her doctor was insisting she take a break somewhere warm over the winter.

'Business has been slow all year, but she's got the chance of a couple of bookings and can't afford to turn them down,' Patricia explained, and Gill almost smiled. Only her mother could make her feel guilty with a few choice words. 'There's a very expensive resort called Mockingbird Farm a couple of miles away, and some guests at an upcoming wedding couldn't get rooms there, so they've talked your aunt into accommodating them.' Patricia sighed. 'It's not much to ask, dear. You know I'd go myself, but . . . ' Her voice trailed away and she wiped at an imaginary tear.

'I know, your heart condition prevents you from flying.' Gill kept to herself the disloyal thought that her mother's health hadn't prevented her from going on a Mediterranean cruise in the summer and dancing the night away. She'd known from the time their conversation started that she'd end up giving in. To stay in Cornwall over Christmas and endure everyone's unspoken sympathy would be unbearable.

'It's only three guests you'd be dealing with, for about four days. The rest of the time all you'd be doing is house-sitting. How hard could it be?' Patricia persisted.

Gill threw up her hands. 'Okay, I'll go. Anything to stop you nagging.'

'I am not — '

'Give in, Mum, while you're winning.' Gill's severe tone worked, as her mother stopped talking, although the satisfied smirk on her face was annoying. 'You can ring Aunt Betsy and tell her I'll come.'

To avoid suffering a bout of her mother's overdone gratitude, she snatched up her coat and briefcase and rushed off to catch the bus to work.

★　★　★

Heavy rain beat against her bedroom window, and the gloomy darkness of the evening suited Gill's mood. She bit back tears as she stared at the empty suitcase opened out on her bed. A couple of weeks ago this had seemed a good idea, but now she was having second thoughts. And third and fourth ones. She wasn't stupid enough to want Michael back, but the future they'd planned together was gone and now she felt like a boat adrift on a stormy sea.

The last week at school had been interminable. She'd gritted her teeth to get through end-of-term exams and all the class parties. It'd taken all Gill's self-control not to snap at her students' irrepressible enthusiasm for the upcoming holidays. To top it off, she'd had to watch Michael walking around with an idiotic grin on his face and gazing adoringly at Stacey Arnold over coffee in the teachers' lounge. The fact the rest of the staff were overly sympathetic to Gill only made things worse. She'd purposely chosen to leave tonight to avoid all the invitations for Christmas drinks. Her coach left St Austell just before ten p.m. and would get her to Heathrow before breakfast tomorrow morning, in good time to catch her noon flight to Charlotte. She'd get a short connecting flight from there on to Knoxville where, Aunt Betsy had assured her, the inn's handyman would be at the airport to meet her.

'Are you nearly done? Our pasties are ready.'

Gill started at the sound of her mother's anxious voice from outside the door. 'Almost. Give me ten minutes and I'll be down. They smell wonderful.'

A lump tightened in her throat as she tried to picture not being here for Christmas. Her older brother and his family always came over for a huge traditional lunch, and they opened their presents together in the afternoon. On Boxing Day her parents threw a big party for all their neighbours and friends. For the first time in all her twenty-seven years, she'd be nearly four thousand miles away for the holidays, and Gill wasn't sure how she felt about that.

This wasn't getting her anywhere. She couldn't let her aunt down, and it would do her good to get away.

She began folding the clothes she'd already selected, and soon zipped her suitcase shut and stood it over by the door. She laid out her documents and money next to her carry-on bag and plugged her phone in to recharge. Before she could think if it was wise, she walked back across the room and opened her top dresser drawer, shifted a jumbled-up pile of socks to one side, and lifted out the white plastic three-ring binder underneath.

She ran her fingers over the girlish handwriting on the front. *Gillian Elizabeth Robinson — Wedding Planner.* For ten years she'd placed her dreams in here, from wedding dress pictures to photos of exotic honeymoon locations, elaborate cake designs, and flower arrangements.

Michael's parting words slammed

back at her: *You've always been more in love with the idea of being married than me. When you can admit that, you'll be a lot happier when you hopefully find the sort of love I've discovered with Stacey.*

It'd taken all her self-control not to scream at him. Gill had trusted him with her love and he'd thrown it back in her face. He didn't get it at all, and that was the saddest part of the whole thing.

For several drawn-out seconds she stared at the file, then at her suitcase, before shoving the offending book back in the dresser. The idea was to leave the sadness behind, not take it with her — apart from the large hole in her heart that she suspected she'd carry around for a long time.

She slammed the drawer shut, straightened her shoulders, and walked back over to the doorway, then picked up her suitcase and headed downstairs. She'd eat her pasty, shed a few tears saying goodbye to her mother, and then set off in search of a new direction.

2

Gill dragged her suitcase along behind her as she scanned the disparate group of people waiting by the arrivals area. She'd no idea what Mr Sawyer looked like, but spotted a solitary older man wearing a checked shirt and denim overalls, and decided to try asking him first. A weary ache pulled at her head, and she frowned as a good-looking businessman suddenly stepped in front of her.

'Miss Gillian Robertson?' His deep, smooth voice took her by surprise, and she could only nod her agreement. 'Luke Sawyer. From the Long River Inn.'

Her hand was seized in a warm, firm grasp, and when she glanced up to meet the stranger's amused gaze she tried not to gape. With his thick, dark hair, lean features and immaculate clothes, Mr

Luke Sawyer was a million miles away from her mental picture of a country inn handyman.

'Don't worry, I've been into Knoxville on business,' he said with a smile. 'I promise I'll fit the image better later. And yes, I know how to use a hammer.' His low, rumbling laugh caught Gill out, and a flush of heat crept up her neck.

'I would assume you do, Mr Sawyer. I'm sure my aunt wouldn't employ you otherwise.' She winced at her haughty tone of voice, but her nemesis only gave in to another sly smile. His bright green eyes swept down over her, and Gill briefly wished she didn't feel so rumpled and travel-stained. She instantly berated herself for caring.

'That's only part of what I do for Miss Betsy.' His enigmatic reply confused her, but she was too tired to question him anymore. Right now all Gill wanted was a decent night's sleep.

'Do you think we could get a move on, Mr Sawyer?' she asked.

'Of course. Your wish is my command.' Luke Sawyer laughingly swept into a low, deep bow, and everyone around stopped what they were doing to stare at them.

'Don't be so ridiculous,' Gill hissed. Before she could sling her small backpack on again, Luke whisked it away and seized her suitcase with his other hand.

He strode off, smiling back over his shoulder at her. 'Come on. It's only about a twenty-minute drive. You can tell me your life story while I try not to scare you on the narrow winding roads.'

'Cornwall has plenty of those. I do believe I'll survive,' she said succinctly, deciding then and there not to tell this man anything.

The moment they stepped outside the airport she shivered, as a blast of cold air hit her straight on.

'Hope you've packed some warmer clothes, because we'll probably get snow over Christmas.' Luke gestured towards her thin black jacket.

'Of course I have.' Gill mentally crossed her fingers that his weather-forecasting skills were wrong. The short, puffy coat in her suitcase wouldn't be much protection in freezing temperatures, but she wasn't about to admit that to Mr Know-it-all.

'Glad to hear it.' His laconic reply sounded like he didn't believe a word she was saying but would humour her for now. 'That's my truck.' He pointed at a huge white vehicle parked by the kerb and set her bags down on the ground next to it.

Gill didn't comment. Anything she might say about the oversized mode of transport with its massive wheels and tinted windows could far too easily be misconstrued, and she wasn't about to give him any more ammunition.

Opening the doors, he turned and nodded to her. 'Hop up in the front.' She headed towards the left door and he briefly touched her arm. 'Other side, honey, unless you're planning to drive us there.' His warm chuckle made her want to smack him. Normally she'd laugh at herself, but her jet-lag headache on top of everything else didn't make her inclined to be amused today. Without replying, she walked around the truck and pulled open the heavy door. She glanced up at the cab and wondered how to get in without falling flat on her face.

'There's a grab handle to help you get up onto the step.'

She followed his instructions without saying another word, and by the time she got herself settled in the passenger seat he'd fitted her suitcase and backpack on the rear bench seat.

'All set?' he asked while reversing and pulling out carefully into traffic. 'So, you've come to help out for a while.'

Gill didn't know how much her aunt had told him, and hoped it wasn't the whole sob story of her cancelled wedding. A gnarled old handyman she could have coped with, but this handsome man with his probing questions and disturbing presence was another story.

'Yes. Betsy needed a break, and I'm free from my teaching job for three weeks over the holidays. I was happy to come to help her and see a part of America I've never seen before.'

He gave her a quick searching stare before turning back to concentrate on the road. 'This isn't your first trip over here?'

She swallowed hard, remembering the holiday to Florida she and Michael took to celebrate their engagement two years earlier. 'I've done the Disneyland thing, that's all.' It hadn't been her choice, but he'd visited multiple times with his family growing up and loved it, so she'd given in.

Luke snorted. 'We'll call this your first time, then. Disney isn't real America any more than people who only visit London can say they've seen England.'

'Fair enough.' Gill couldn't help laughing.

'I sure am glad to hear you've got a sense of humour in there somewhere,' he teased, and she didn't know how to reply without coming across as prissy.

She glanced out of the window and seized hold of the door handle as she stared with her mouth gaping open at the steep mountainside dropping away from her vision beneath them. The last vestiges of late-afternoon light exposed just enough of the bare wintery view to intimidate anyone used to a softer landscape.

'Exactly like your Cornish roads, is it?' Luke joked, irony running through his voice.

'Not quite.'

'I tried to warn you.' His easy manner was irritating. 'Don't worry. We'll soon be heading down into Walland.' Gill didn't want to admire the competent way he steered them into the next sharp bend and out the other side. 'It takes a while to appreciate the starker beauty at this time of year. Most visitors come in the fall for the colours. You won't believe how stunning it is then.'

'Maybe I'll get the chance to come back to visit my aunt again,' she replied.

Luke gave her a strange look. 'Yeah. Maybe.'

Gill glanced back out of the window and saw they were crossing over a narrow stone bridge. She admired the neat buildings on either side and noticed there were few of the gaudy signs Florida had been inundated with. Instead there were Christmas lights everywhere, with even the smallest homes adorned with colourful eye-catching decorations — everything from inflatable reindeer to large nativity scenes in the front gardens. 'Goodness, you really like Christmas here, don't you?'

'I guess.' By his indifferent tone Gill took a wild guess Mr Sawyer wasn't a fan. 'The town here was started to provide accommodations for workers at a tannery that's now long gone,' he carried on, obviously not planning to continue the Christmas discussion. 'When people started coming to visit the Smoky Mountains around the beginning of the twentieth century, it helped the economy, and that's what we rely on now. We're about a ten-minute drive from the park, but luckily we're far enough from Gatlinburg and Pigeon Forge that we haven't been exploited in the same way. Of course, give us time and we'll probably ruin this too.'

His cynicism startled her and Gill didn't know how to reply.

'Sorry. I'm not supposed to get on my hobby horse the minute you arrive. Betsy would tell me off if she was here.'

'What do you mean, if she was here?' Gill said with a touch of panic.

'I assumed she told you.' An enigmatic smile crept across his face. 'I was doing double duty at the airport. I dropped Betsy off for her flight to Dallas. She'll connect through there to Miami.' As he spoke, he indicated and turned the truck onto a narrow road.

Gill was just able to make out a river to her left, and tried to concentrate on that rather than thinking about Luke

Sawyer's bombshell.

'Don't worry. I've got my own small cottage at the back of the inn.'

She didn't know whether to be relieved or even more apprehensive. She had been relying on her aunt to get her settled into the routine of running the inn before she left. Talk about being dropped in at the deep end.

'Here she is. The Long River Inn. You'll appreciate her more in the morning when you can see better.' He steered along a curved gravel driveway and brought the truck to a stop.

Gill slowly undid her seatbelt and opened the door. Remembering just in time about the deep drop, she carefully stepped down and stretched out her aching back as she stared at the charming building in front of her. The pictures hadn't done it justice at all. Gill fell in love.

3

'Gotcha.' Luke came to join her. 'It did the same to me the day I arrived.'

'You didn't grow up around here, then?' She'd caught hints of a soft drawl in his voice and assumed he was local to the area.

'No.' The terse reply took her by surprise. 'I'm sorry. I didn't intend to be rude.' Luke's quick smile didn't quite cover up the fact he didn't want to talk about himself. She needed to respect that.

Gill glanced away and concentrated on having a proper look at the inn. The myriad glittering white lights strung across the roof, the gleaming candle-shaped lights in every window, and fresh evergreen wreath on the front door all emphasized the beauty of the old building. She loved the traditional southern design with the gabled upstairs windows, white wood siding and wraparound porch. It was far larger than she'd imagined.

'Are there any guests at the moment?' She didn't consider herself easily scared, but the idea of staying here alone was daunting.

'Only one. Mr Walton is an older gentleman who comes several times a year to hike in the park. He's leaving tomorrow, and on Monday your wedding guests arrive to stay for a couple of nights.' Another quirky smile tugged at Luke's mouth. 'Of course, you won't ever be lonely with Ella McBride around.'

'Dare I ask who she is?' Gill asked cautiously.

Luke shifted closer and she caught a hint of his warm, woodsy cologne. 'Ella is the Long River Inn's resident ghost. I can't believe Betsy didn't mention her. Some say she's the tragic young widow of the first owner. Of course, there are others who go for the murder story . . . '

'Murder?' Gill's voice rose.

'Her father refused to let her marry

the local blacksmith and locked her in the house to stop her from running away. She was never seen again, but Ella's moans have woken many a guest from a good night's sleep.' Luke's warm breath heated her skin. 'Of course, people like me think it's all a load of nonsense, and only repeat the story to amuse gullible tourists.'

Gill jerked away. 'You are a very annoying man. I'd like to go inside please, resident ghost or not.'

A flash of humour lit up his eyes before he simply nodded and picked up her bags again. He walked over to the porch steps and headed on up, leaving her to follow along behind him.

'There's no better place around to drink your morning coffee, even in this chilly weather. It's worth dressing up warmly for.' He gestured towards the rocking chairs interspersed with small tables spaced out along the porch.

'I would imagine I'll be too busy,' Gill replied.

'Get up earlier.'

She ignored his sly dig and stepped around him to walk across to the inn's front door. 'Is it unlocked?'

'Yep. Mr Walton was here when I left for the airport and said he'd keep an eye on things while I was gone. Betsy and I always try to make sure one of us is around the property.'

Gill opened the door and stepped straight into a large open room wonderfully scented by a beautifully decorated live Christmas tree. Its white lights glittered and sparkled, and the gold star on the top almost reached the ceiling. The tree stood to one side of a stone fireplace, where blazing logs sent out a welcome blast of warmth. Across the mantelpiece there were swaths of greenery looped up with red bows, and above stood elegant groupings of plain creamy white candles, their soft glow adding to the general ambiance. She glanced around the rest of the room and admired the polished dark wood floors and plain white walls decorated with framed old photos. Everything suited the gracious old house, and she couldn't wait to explore.

'Welcome to the Long River Inn, my dear.' A white-haired man rose to his feet and placed the book he'd been reading back down on the low table in front of him. 'Thaddeus Walton at your service.'

Gill stifled a smile at his old-fashioned language. 'I'm pleased to meet you.' She stepped forward and shook his outstretched hand.

'I'm very sorry about your aunt. She's a wonderful woman, and . . . ' Staring behind her, Mr. Walton suddenly went quiet. For some reason Luke had warned him off continuing. 'I'm leaving in the morning after breakfast, but if I can help you in any way until then, please don't hesitate to ask. And don't trouble yourself fixing me a full breakfast. A couple of sausage biscuits will do, and a pot of coffee.'

Why any biscuit recipe would include sausage, and why anyone would want it for breakfast, was beyond her. She'd have to swallow her pride later and ask

Luke what Mr Walton was talking about. For now she'd at least try to give the impression that she knew what she was doing. 'Of course. What time would you care for breakfast?'

Mr Walton smiled. 'Eight is your aunt's regular time, and that has always been perfectly acceptable to me. If you'll excuse me, I'll be going along to bed now. Goodnight, my dear.' He gave a polite nod and picked up his book before heading toward the stairs.

An uneasy silence fell in the room as they were left alone. Gill guessed Luke expected her to ask about the earlier conversation but decided not to give him the satisfaction. She had the patience to wait, and instead turned to him with a bright smile. 'I don't suppose you have any clue what I'm supposed to do in the morning?'

'I sure do.' His amused tone got to her. She couldn't imagine why she was supposed to assume the handyman would be up to speed on the running of the kitchen.

'Good. If you wouldn't mind showing me that first, then maybe you can take me to where I'll be sleeping. Tomorrow you can give me a full tour of the inn when I'm more awake.' She spoke in the same firm way as she did to a class full of stroppy teenagers, needing to establish her position before they went any further.

'Yes, ma'am.' Luke nodded and his slow smile convinced her he knew exactly what she was doing. He slipped off his suit jacket and hung it on the back of the nearest chair. She wished he'd kept it on, because something about the broad stretch of his back under the slim-fitting shirt made her more aware of his physical presence. 'Betsy always sets breakfast up out here.' He pointed to two long rectangular tables over by the door, their dark wood gleaming after years of loving polishing. 'She serves the food in large dishes, family-style, so the guests can eat together and chat.'

'Won't poor Mr Walton be rather lost

there on his own in the morning?'

'When she doesn't have many guests, Betsy normally joins them with a cup of coffee, unless they've made it plain they don't want company.' His eyes twinkled as they rested on Gill. 'I'm pretty sure Thaddeus will be happy to bend your ear talking about all aspects of the park, if you give him half a chance.'

'Where's the kitchen?' She wondered how much longer she could keep her culinary ignorance under wraps. Normally Gill would cheerfully admit when she didn't know something and ask questions, but something about Luke Sawyer made her reluctant to do that today.

'Through here.' He headed towards the back of the room and opened a door before stepping to one side and gesturing for her to go ahead of him.

She stepped into a generously sized modern kitchen with gleaming stainless-steel appliances and sparkling white countertops. 'Oh. It's not what I expected.' She had erroneously imagined well-worn pine fixtures and country-style decorations, along with outdated equipment.

Luke grinned. 'Nope, don't suppose it is.' A sudden shadow flitted across his eyes. 'This was Hank's last present to Betsy before he passed away. He oversaw the remodelling even when he was sick, and made sure everything was exactly as she wanted. Now I'm not sure . . . ' His voice trailed away and he stared down at the floor.

The breath caught in Gill's throat, and she wondered if she might find out what was going on with her aunt. She fixed her gaze on him and waited.

4

Luke glanced back up and met her curiosity without flinching. 'You're in luck. Betsy took pity on you and fixed a ton of food before leaving. It's all in the freezer. If we get some biscuits out to defrost, you'll only have to pop them in a warm oven for a few minutes in the morning, and Thaddeus will never know you didn't make them with your own fair hands. You'll have to fry up the sausage, but I'm guessing you can manage that.'

'How do you know I'm not an accomplished cook?' She tossed the question out and he instantly burst out laughing, the deep, warm sound filling the room.

'Come on, sweetheart, it doesn't take half a brain to work that one out.' Luke flashed a wide smile. 'The biggest clue was the way you went mighty pale when the breakfast menu was mentioned. I'm also guessing you're imagining trying to serve delicate English tea biscuits with a side order of sausage, and have decided southerners are more than a touch peculiar.'

A rush of heat flamed Gill's cheeks. No matter how much she wanted to dispute his observations, the streak of honesty running through her wouldn't let her lie outright, so she held her tongue.

'Our biscuits are kind of similar to your scones, except they aren't sweet,' Luke explained. 'We eat them for breakfast with sausage or country ham, and also with butter and honey or preserves. Of course, most true southerners will happily eat them with any meal. There's nothing better than good fried chicken with green beans, coleslaw, fried apples, and a side order of fresh biscuits,' he expounded, and his enthusiasm for the food shone through.

'Right,' Gill said faintly. 'But when the other guests are here, I'm sure they'll expect more than Mr Walton requested.'

'Afraid so, honey.' Luke opened a drawer and pulled out a well-thumbed black leather book. He laid it on the counter. 'This is Betsy's recipe book. She plans the menus for the whole week so people get something different every day.'

Anyone can fry a bit of bacon. Gill remembered her mother's blithe words with a sinking heart.

Luke strode across the room and opened one door of a huge fridge-freezer whose top almost touched the ceiling. He pulled out two large foil-covered pans and peered at the labels. 'This one here is a hashbrown casserole, and the other is Betsy's famous western omelette casserole. There's several each of those, plus a couple of her delicious bourbon French toast recipe, and the winter fruit compote.' He returned them to the freezer and pointed to a large cardboard box on the next shelf down. 'Those are frozen sausage patties. Fry them gently for about ten minutes in one of the cast-iron skillets.'

Gill wasn't sure what a cast-iron skillet even looked like, but admitting that was going too far.

'Don't fret. Tomorrow I'll go through everything in more detail,' Luke said, as though that was supposed to reassure her. 'I sure hope you can make decent coffee. Most folks will forgive you anything if you're okay with that.'

Somehow she had the idea pouring boiling water over instant coffee granules wasn't what he had in mind, and shook her head.

'Heck, woman, what do you normally exist on?' He sounded exasperated. 'Teabags and hot water, I'm guessing.'

Gill gave an apologetic shrug.

'Come over here.' He beckoned her over to join him and pointed to the imposing stainless-steel machine standing on the counter. 'It's real simple. Water goes in there. Filter and coffee in there.' He gestured to the appropriate spots and Gill struggled to pay attention through her increasing jet-lag fog. 'Measurements are here on the machine, so you can't go wrong. Turn it on a good thirty minutes before you want it ready.' He pointed to the stainless-steel flasks on the counter. 'Fill up one of these to take out to the table so it'll stay good and hot.' Suddenly he turned and frowned at her. 'You're exhausted. None of this is sinking in, is it?'

She tried for a cheerful smile. 'We'll find out in the morning, won't we?'

'I can come in early and give you a hand, if you want,' Luke offered, and for a second she wavered. It would be so easy to agree, but she needed to stand on her own two feet.

She gently pulled away. 'No, thank you.' They continued to look at each other, and it was hard to keep her gaze steady under the power of Luke's clear green eyes.

'Fair enough. Betsy's put you in her rooms, so I'll show you where things

are and get on back to my own place.'
He turned away and headed back out
to the other room. Gill followed and
silently trailed after him as he took her
bags and led the way down a long
hallway off the main room. He stopped
at the far end and opened a sturdy
wood door. The cold night air hit Gill,
taking her breath away for a few
seconds.

'She doesn't live in the main house?'

'Nope,' Luke replied shortly. 'Let's
go this way.' They went down a narrow,
well-lit path partially covered by a
corrugated roof fixed to an open wood
frame. 'Betsy and Hank had a small
house built behind the garage to give
them some privacy. There's an internal
phone connection so guests can contact
them overnight if they have any
problems.'

Gill's unease increased as they
reached a small bungalow built of plain
concrete blocks and with little to soften
its simple design. 'Oh, right.'

'If you're uncomfortable here, you

can sleep in one of the spare guest bedrooms. It probably didn't occur to Betsy you might find it a tad isolated.' He set down her bags outside the door and touched her arm. As the warmth from his fingers seeped through her jacket, Gill wished more than anything he wouldn't move away too soon.

'I'll be fine.'

He shifted closer and touched a finger to her jaw, tilting her face so she couldn't avoid his searching gaze. 'I'm guessin' this is the British stiff upper lip in action?' The touch of teasing in his deep, soft voice got to her and she blinked away a rush of tired tears.

She took a step backwards, and Luke's hands dropped away. 'Absolutely. May I have the key, please?' she said in a brisk tone, and hoped he'd get the hint.

'Do you want me to come in and show you — '

'No, thank you,' Gill cut him off. 'I'll see you in the morning, and thanks for all your help.' She held out her hand,

and with a distinct touch of reluctance he fished a key out of his pocket and passed it over. Steeling herself to ignore the warm brush of his skin as their fingers touched, she thanked him again and turned to unlock the door.

'Sleep well.' He walked away, and as he disappeared out of sight Gill almost yelled at him to come back. The icy darkness wrapped around her and she heard nothing except her own heartbeat thumping against her chest. Before she could lose her nerve, she shoved the key in and turned it quickly, throwing open the door and fumbling around for a light switch.

She sagged against the wall with relief as a surge of brightness lit up the comfortable room in front of her. She picked up her bags and hauled them inside before dropping them down again to have a proper look around.

The compact living room was warmly decorated in welcoming shades of cream and yellow. It was also decorated for Christmas, but with the jumbled-up style of mismatched ornaments and coloured lights her own mother preferred. Gill's throat tightened as she pictured their own gaudy artificial tree complete with badly made ornaments from her childhood. *Get a grip. You aren't going to spend the next couple of weeks feeling sorry for yourself.*

Instead of wallowing in useless self-pity, she walked over to a square antique oak table next to the sofa and picked up the silver-framed photo standing in the middle. It contained the same picture her aunt had sent to them last Christmas. Taken on the front porch of the inn, it showed her aunt and uncle wrapped in a tight hug and smiling at each other. A wave of sadness swept through Gill — partly for Betsy and Hank, who'd lost something special, but also for herself because she wanted what they'd had.

She brushed away a tear. *Gillian Elizabeth, get to bed.* Her mother's admonition rang out loud and clear. *A good night's sleep and everything will seem better in the morning.*

Of course she'd still be faced with the prospect of cooking the mysterious sausage, and dealing with the enigmatic Luke Sawyer, but maybe after eight hours of uninterrupted sleep neither would seem as daunting. She could only hope.

5

Gill stared at the fossilized black lumps of sausage in the bottom of the pan and bit back a curse. Last night's dream of eight hours' sleep had turned into a sad joke, and she'd spent the hours from two until five wide awake and staring at the ceiling. Naturally she'd then sunk into a bone-weary slumber and was startled when the alarm clock rang at seven o'clock. After the quickest shower of her life, she'd made her way to the kitchen, and within ten minutes felt like crawling back under the bedcovers.

Finding the cast-iron skillet proved the least of her worries, as the heavy black frying pan had been tucked inside the oven ready to use. The industrial-sized oven was another story. By the time she worked out how to turn on the stupid thing, her chances of getting breakfast ready on time were fast receding.

Gill had set the pan on one of the large rings to heat, then tackled the coffee machine. She'd taken eight slices of sausage out of the freezer and tossed them into the hot pan, having to jump back when it splattered like crazy. Within a few minutes the meat turned into the cremated remnants in front of her. She stood and mused over what to do next. If she put more sausage in, would the same thing happen again?

Mr Walton suddenly burst in through the swing door. 'Goodness, my dear, what on earth are you doing? I think we'd better turn the fan on.' Gill watched helplessly as he flicked a switch over the oven to clear the haze of smoke hanging over them. 'Is there any more sausage?' he asked with a kind smile. She pulled herself together and nodded, quickly going to fetch the box from the freezer.

'The first thing we need to do is turn the heat down.' Mr Walton altered the temperature and carried the pan over to dump the burnt sausage into the bin.

He grabbed a handful of paper towels from a roll on the wall and methodically started to wipe out the pan. 'Never use soap and water on cast iron or you'll spoil the finish. Your aunt has seasoned this one over many years.'

Gill didn't like to comment on how unhygienic that sounded.

'Sausage does best put if you start it off in a cold skillet and then cook it slowly over medium heat.'

She had a vague memory of Luke trying to tell her some of this last night, but it'd obviously gone in one ear and out the other. 'Thank you so much.'

'It's not a problem, my girl. I always cooked breakfast for my dear late wife. What about the biscuits?' he asked.

Gill blushed and pointed to the defrosted biscuits still sitting on a baking tin. 'I'm afraid I didn't make them myself.'

'Good,' he replied with a distinct twinkle in his pale blue eyes. 'We might be safe, then. Do you have the oven turned on?'

'Yes, but I don't know how hot it's supposed to be.'

He bent down to check the knob and fiddled with it before opening the door and placing the biscuits on one of the racks. 'Very low. These are already cooked, so you're only wanting to warm them through.'

'I've made the coffee,' she declared hopefully, and crossed her fingers behind her back as he left the gently sizzling sausage alone to check the coffee machine.

Mr Walton filled one of the mugs she'd set out and took a sip. Gill held her breath and waited for the verdict, relieved beyond speech when a satisfied smile crept over his face.

'Well, we've discovered something you can do in the kitchen, so let's celebrate and eat breakfast together.' He filled one of the coffee pots and held it out to her. 'Why don't you pop that in the other room while I see to the food. Have you got butter and honey set out on the table?'

'Yes, I did manage that,' she said ruefully. 'At least, I hope so. I'm not sure even I could mess that up.' Mr Walton burst out laughing and she joined in, feeling instantly better.

Five minutes later, Gill was enjoying herself more than she had in years. Aunt Betsy's biscuits were delicious, buttery and soft, and with the spicy sausage made the most unique breakfast she'd ever eaten. Combined with a large mug of good strong coffee, she began to feel almost human again.

Mr Walton was a fascinating story-teller, exactly as Luke had promised. The historian in her loved hearing his tales of the first settlers in Tennessee and the way the Great Smoky Mountains became such a draw first for serious hikers and later the tourist attraction they were today. She suspected he knew more about the town of Walland and the Long River Inn than most locals ever would, and only wished her guest were staying longer.

The front door burst open and Luke

strolled in, bringing with him a blast of the cold early-morning air. Gill tried not to stare, but it was a challenge. In well-worn jeans, a soft flannel shirt and scuffed work boots, he looked even more tempting this morning.

'Is there any decent coffee going, or did she manage to burn it?' He gave Mr Walton a conspiratorial wink, then pulled out the chair closest to Gill and sat down, resting one foot up on his other leg. *Smug, self-satisfied creature*, she thought. Thankfully, the comment had tossed a much-needed mental bucket of cold water over her inexplicable attraction to him.

Mr Walton didn't say a word; only reached for one of the empty mugs and filled it with coffee from the pot. He pushed it towards Luke. 'I believe you'll find it's excellent, and no, I didn't help the young lady make it.'

She didn't dare catch Luke's eye. He wasn't lying, but he wasn't exactly being truthful either.

Luke took a deep, satisfied swallow

and looked back across at her. 'My apologies. I underestimated you.'

Not really. Gill almost blurted out the story of the sausage disaster, but Mr Walton caught her eye and shook his head behind Luke's back.

'We've eaten our fill if you're hungry.' Mr Walton waved his hand over the plate of remaining sausage biscuits, and Gill took another sip of coffee to stop from laughing out loud.

'Thanks.' Luke grabbed one and took a large bite. In a couple of mouthfuls it was gone, and he grinned at her. 'So you do know your way about a kitchen better than you let on last night. Clever girl.'

She couldn't decide whether to laugh or cry. If she continued this charade he'd think she didn't need any help, and then she'd be sunk when it came to the more complicated breakfasts. But if she admitted the truth now, she'd be showing up her wonderful guest and giving Luke Sawyer more to aggravate her about for the rest of her time here.

'It never pays to reveal everything from the start, does it?' she replied, crossing her fingers under the table.

'Certainly doesn't, sweetheart.' He tossed her a laconic smile and toyed with his coffee mug, swinging it gently around on the table. 'I guess that means you won't need any advice on the evening desserts, either.' He fixed his attention back on Mr Walton. 'Did you tell our temporary innkeeper about Betsy's special daily treat for her guests?'

Gill caught a glimpse of unease on Mr Walton's face before it returned to his usual friendly smile. 'I don't believe I did, but I'm sure Gillian will cope admirably.'

She wanted to ask what on earth he was talking about, but made herself sit still and continue to sip coffee as though she wasn't bothered about a single thing. Luke held her fast with his sharp gaze, and she knew now what a butterfly stuck through with a pin must feel like as it struggled to get free. 'Do tell me, Mr Sawyer — I can tell you're dying to,' Gill said as casually as she could manage.

'Betsy always has a homemade dessert ready for her guests about eight o'clock each night. They're welcome to gather and chat over coffee. Many people say it's their favourite part of their stay,' he explained with more than a hint of amusement.

'What a wonderful idea.' She plastered on a bright smile.

Luke didn't comment; only pushed back his chair and stood up. 'If you want the grand tour I'll give it to you now, before I start work.'

She didn't ask exactly what his work involved, and presumed he wouldn't be looking to her for instructions. Somehow she imagined Luke had his own agenda and would follow it without reference to anyone or anything. Where her aunt had discovered him, and why he was content to work here, was a mystery she was determined to solve. The man who'd greeted her at the airport was no ordinary handyman, no matter how much he pretended to be.

'That would be perfect. I'll clear up breakfast first, if you don't mind.' It wasn't meant to be a question, and she didn't wait for a reply. 'Mr Walton, is there anything else I can get you?'

'No, thank you, my dear. I'm going to pack so I can be on my way soon,' he replied.

'Do you have a long drive home?' Gill asked as she started to stack the dirty dishes on the wooden tray they'd carried their breakfast in on earlier.

'No.' Mr Walton shook his head. 'It's about three hours to Nashville without stops, although I always break the journey around Crossville. My little car could make it by itself, I've done the journey so many times.'

'Let me know when you have your suitcase packed and I'll be happy to bring it downstairs for you,' Luke offered.

'That's very kind of you, my boy, but it won't be necessary. I don't have much to carry,' he said firmly before turning back to Gill. 'I'll stop to see you and say my farewells before I leave.'

Mr Walton headed for the stairs and Luke rolled his eyes playfully at her. 'Your aunt tried to put him in one of the downstairs rooms last time and he got quite offended. He said while he was still able to walk up to the top of Clingman's Dome, he could manage one flight of stairs.' He chuckled. 'Clingman's Dome is a very steep hike not far away from here, and it's not for the faint-hearted.'

'I'm sure he knows his own limits. I suggest we make a start so we can both get busy with our day's work.' Gill knew she sounded like a typical school-teacher, but it was her only form of protection against the pull he had on her — an attraction she definitely didn't need.

Luke's smiling eyes darkened but he didn't say a word; only grabbed the coffee pot and strode off towards the kitchen without a backward glance.

With a sigh she finished loading the tray and followed him. Hopefully they'd get this over with quickly and he could get back to doing whatever a handyman did. Then she could worry about the myriad other things sent to try her. So much for getting away from her problems — all she'd done was swap one set for another.

6

Gill could blame her spinning head on jet lag, but rather thought it was due to Luke's whirlwind kitchen tour. Due to his mistaken impression of her culinary abilities, he'd raced through his explanations, leaving her to smile brightly and nod at regular intervals as if she had a clue what he was talking about.

'Are you good with all that?' he asked in his usual challenging way.

'I think so.' How hard could it be? She had Aunt Betsy's recipe books, the ability to read, and vague memories of school cookery classes. And there was always the internet — the source of all wisdom.

'Fine. Let's have a tour of the rest of the house, and then I'll leave you to it.'

'Perfect.' She tried to sound convincing.

'Let's start upstairs and work our

way down,' he announced, and set off out of the kitchen.

Gill followed along, and on the way up the curved staircase she couldn't help hanging back and studying the fascinating photos on the walls.

'All the pictures you see around the house are either of the inn at various stages in its history or of the town. You can look at them to your heart's content later.'

In other words, don't waste my time now. Gill almost stuck out her tongue at his retreating back, but he'd be bound to turn and catch her out.

When they entered the long, narrow hallway, Luke pulled out a large ring of keys from his pocket and selected one. 'This is the Helena Suite, named after the wife of the man who built the inn.' He opened the door and stood back to let her go in first.

She glanced around the generously sized room, admiring the rich burgundy and cream decor that complemented the Victorian mahogany furniture. Her aunt had fixed up a small Christmas tree here, too, complete with old-fashioned ornaments, and had also grouped a collection of antique lace angels on the top of the dresser.

'They've all got pretty much the same amenities,' Luke explained. 'Queen-sized beds — except for a king in one of the downstairs suites, private bathrooms, and a small sitting area. This one has the best view of the river.' He crossed the room and opened back one of the French doors. 'Come and see.'

She joined him on a small balcony barely wide enough to contain two wrought-iron chairs. 'Gosh. I didn't realize last night how close we are to the river.'

Just across the narrow road in front of the inn was the Long River, sparkling in today's wintery sunshine. The trees were bare now, but it wasn't hard to imagine how pretty they'd be in the spring. A quick blast of cold wind made her shiver, and she gave a start as Luke slid an arm around her shoulders.

'Sorry. I forgot you weren't wearing

much,' he murmured.

She glanced up to meet his open, frank stare, suddenly aware of how revealing her long-sleeved silky T-shirt was. She pulled away and quickly ran back inside. When he joined her, it was with an amused smile plastered all over his handsome face.

'Why don't I look at the other bedrooms up here later when I clean Mr Walton's room?' she suggested. Anything to avoid being in this man's disturbing company for any longer than necessary.

'Fair enough.' He gave an easy shrug. 'Betsy usually gets Mary Lou Beard from the town in to help out, but she's busy with her family over the holidays, so you're on your own I'm afraid.'

'It's not a problem.' She'd rather have plenty of things to fill her time, and wielding a duster and cleaning a couple of bathrooms would be a cinch compared to cooking.

'You ready to go back down?' he asked and she nodded, leaving him to lead the way. At the bottom of the stairs he pointed towards the corridor leading to her own accommodation. 'The other two guest rooms are down there. You'll see there's another small seating area on the right, too. There are games and books for guests to help themselves to while they're here.' He turned back to face the main room again. 'The TV over there by the tree is the only one available for the guests to use.'

She saw him glance at his watch — a heavy, good-quality one she couldn't help noticing earlier. 'Am I keeping you from your other tasks?'

Luke's mouth turned up in amusement at her ham-fisted attempt to probe. 'Yep, but it's okay. Betsy instructed me to help you as much as possible,' he announced with a teasing smile. 'If you notice anything that needs to be fixed when you're around the place, just let me know. I'll be in the Kingsley Suite installing a new shower if you're looking for me. It's the closest one to the outside door.'

For the life of her, Gill still couldn't see this as a full-time job for a young, active man, but kept her mouth shut. 'Thank you for everything.' Before he could reply, she swung around on her heels and walked away.

* * *

Gill pored over her aunt's recipe book and sighed. The simplest dessert she could find was something called an apple crisp, which appeared to resemble the fruit crumbles she was familiar with back home. After reading it through for the third time, she decided it would have to do.

A heavy thumping noise from some-where outside the kitchen startled her, and she jumped up from her chair. She headed for the door, and as she flung it open she heard loud moaning sounds and hesitated, her heart thumping like crazy.

You won't ever be lonely with Ella McBride around.

Luke's words came back to haunt her. Haunt her? Gill clapped her hand across her mouth to stifle a scream but instantly dropped it back down to her side. Somehow she didn't think the mythical Ella McBride would know her name, and it was definitely her name she heard being called in a distinctly masculine voice.

'Gillian, my dear — I need your help.'

She gazed frantically around, and now she did scream. Running across the room, she dropped to her knees on the floor next to Mr Walton. 'Oh, my goodness. Whatever have you done?' He lay in a heap at the bottom of the stairs, his face as white as any supposed ghost. She noticed his right arm was twisted awkwardly under him.

'I should have listened to Mr Sawyer,' he tried to explain through heavy, strained breaths. 'It was my own silly fault.'

'Not at all,' she said soothingly. 'I'll go and get Luke.'

Mr Walton rested his head back against the lowest stair and closed his eyes. 'That's an excellent idea, my dear.'

Gill scrambled to her feet and raced off down the hall, then flung open the door to the Kingsley Suite. 'Luke, please come quickly. Mr Walton's fallen down the stairs, and I don't know what to do, and . . . '

In a matter of seconds he was in front of her, grasping her shoulders with his strong hands and fixing her with his calm, steady gaze. 'Slow down and say it again, honey. I was in the bathroom and only caught a word or two.' He frowned and nodded as she repeated the story. 'Come on.' He seized her hand and dragged her with him as he hurried back down the hallway.

'Oughtn't we call for an ambulance?' she asked.

'Hang on a sec.' He squeezed her hand in reassurance before letting go and hurrying over to their injured guest. He squatted down beside him and didn't touch him immediately, asking brief questions and paying close attention to the answers. Then he gently manipulated the man's injured hand and then shifted down to look at the right ankle the man was pointing to.

'I'm sorry to be so much trouble. I should have — '

'Please don't talk that way, sir. It was an accident,' Luke said kindly, and stood back up. 'Your wrist could be broken, but I'm pretty sure the ankle injury is only a sprain and just needs strapping up. If you're agreeable, I'll pop you in my truck and run you to the hospital. It'll get you there faster than waiting for an ambulance to get all the way out here.'

'Are you sure that's a good idea?' Gill couldn't resist interrupting.

'It most certainly is, my dear,' Mr Walton declared. 'I have faith in Mr Sawyer.'

She caught a glance pass between the two men, something understood but unspoken.

'I'll go and bring the truck around to

the front door and then come back to carry you out,' Luke said, and then looked back at Gill. 'If you could get a couple of pillows and a blanket from his room, I'll be able to make him more comfortable.'

'Of course.' She headed back up the stairs, and as she disappeared out of sight heard a murmured conversation going on. She couldn't make out what was being said, but it made her even more curious.

Five minutes later she stood at the front door and waved them off, equally worried about Mr Walton and the idea of attempting to make an edible apple crisp.

7

Gill held the small, sharp knife in her hand and wondered how Aunt Betsy defined a thin slice of apple. Once Luke and Mr Walton had gone, she'd avoided the kitchen and had an in-depth look around the inn. She had got so engrossed in looking at all the old photographs that a couple of hours soon flew by. Half an hour ago she had forced herself to tackle tonight's dessert, but so far peeling and coring four apples was as far as she'd got.

Luke stuck his head in around the kitchen door. 'Everything all right?'

'Of course. Why wouldn't it be?' she replied with an assurance she didn't feel. 'More importantly, how is Mr Walton?'

'Doing as fine as a nearly seventy-year-old man with a fractured wrist and sprained ankle can be.' He ambled in and pulled out one of the kitchen stools to sit on. 'I've put him down in the Kingsley Suite so he won't have to manage the stairs. The shower's fixed, and the whole bathroom is accessible for the disabled. You can put some of the wedding guests up in his old room instead. I checked, and they didn't particularly request the downstairs rooms. I think Betsy chose to put them there so it would be less going up and down the stairs for her.'

Gill almost asked if he thought he was running the place, but knew it would sound ungrateful.

'I've come in now to fix him some coffee and a sandwich for lunch — if that's okay with you, of course,' Luke said with a smirk. A rush of heat travelled up Gill's neck, no doubt lighting up her face like a flashing red light. 'Let me do it for you.' She set down her knife, but Luke reached across and touched her arm, the press of his firm fingers disconcerting her yet again. 'You carry on with what you're doing, and I'll put lunch together for all of us. I'll have mine in with Mr Walton. It'll keep him company, and I can monitor how he's doing without making it too obvious.'

He let go of her and stood up to go over to the fridge, then opened the door and pulled out various containers. 'Will turkey on wheat bread work for you?'

'Perfect.' She made herself turn back to her apples and picked up the knife again to start. Slowly and methodically, she worked her way through the pile, and when she was done tossed them all in the dish she had ready. She glanced furtively in Luke's direction, noticing how competently he worked, and guessed he'd have the same confidence in everything he did. She forced herself to check the recipe and measured out what she hoped was the right amount of brown sugar and cinnamon before stirring the sweet mixture into the apples.

'You might stop by to see Mr Walton later,' Luke suggested. 'I could do with you backing me up to persuade him to stay over Christmas. Even if he could get home, there's no one there to help him out.' Concern ran through his voice, and Gill couldn't help softening.

'Of course. It didn't occur to me, I'm afraid.'

'No worries,' he replied, deftly slicing tomatoes so fast Gill knew she'd be fingerless if she attempted to emulate him. 'Apart from anything else, the weather forecast isn't looking great.'

'Oh. I haven't been paying attention.' She frowned.

'Part of the job.'

The thought ran through her mind that everything appeared to be part of Luke's job, from what she'd seen so far. She reached for the mixing bowl and scale, and searched for the flour she knew she'd got out earlier.

Luke shared out the sandwiches between their three plates and added large slices of pickle on the side, then a heap of thick-cut crisps. 'All set. You want me to leave yours here?'

Gill nodded. 'I need to get this in the oven before I stop to eat.'

'You might want to turn it on first.'

'I wasn't ready, so I didn't want to do it too early,' Gill said defensively, not wanting to admit she'd forgotten that important step.

He shrugged. 'Up to you.' He reached under the counter and lifted up a large wooden tray, then loaded it up with the two plates and carried it back over to the fridge. 'I'm taking a couple of sodas for us. There's homemade lemonade, or sweet tea if you prefer.' He picked up the tray and left without another word, leaving Gill gratefully alone again. Everything about him disturbed her, from his physical presence to his sharp observations and general competence at absolutely everything. She'd love to discover something Luke Sawyer wasn't good at.

Half an hour later she finally had the dish in the oven, and collapsed onto one of the stools, totally exhausted. For a woman who could handle a classroom full of rowdy teenage boys with her hands tied behind her back, this was pathetic. Anyone would think she'd prepared a ten-course banquet for a hundred people instead of one sad apple pie. She'd set the timer for half an hour; Betsy's recipe said thirty to forty minutes, so she'd check then and babysit it until the pie turned what her aunt called golden-brown and bubbling.

Too tired to bother getting up again to fetch a drink, she simply grabbed a sandwich and crammed it into her mouth. She didn't know what Luke had added, but this tasted so much better than her regular lunchtime efforts. She pulled back the bread and noticed chopped fresh herbs on top of the tomato slices and a thicker and creamier version of mayonnaise than she was used to. She munched away and soon cleared the plate. Pushing it to one side, she rested her head on her folded arms and let her eyes close for a minute.

'Are you trying to burn the place down?'

Gill jerked upright and barely managed to stop herself from toppling off of the stool. A loud alarm was ringing, and through a haze of smoke she watched Luke yank something out of the oven and throw it down on the counter.

'You took the title apple crisp seriously, didn't you, sweetheart?' He chuckled and hurried to open the back door leading out to the garden. The fresh cold air helped to clear away the smoke, and the alarm thankfully stopped.

'Oh, my goodness. What happened?' She peered at the smouldering remains of her dessert.

'At a wild guess, I'd say you fell asleep. I could be totally wrong, but this cremated offering and your pink creased face sort of indicate that's the case.' He touched her cheek and she jerked away.

'But I set the timer. I know I did,' Gill protested.

Luke shook his head. 'That's my fault. I should've told you it didn't work. I'm really sorry, honey.' The faint lines on his forehead deepened. 'Betsy wouldn't let me fix it. She said she didn't ever use it and preferred to cook by instinct, knowing when food was ready by how it smelled.'

'If that's the criteria, I'd say this is cooked, wouldn't you?' Gill joked, dramatically sniffing at the overdone pie. She reached up and squeezed his shoulder. 'It's okay, don't worry. It's only the three of us. I'm sure Mr Walton won't complain, and I'll hopefully get it right before our other guests arrive.'

'I'll fix the timer when the oven's cooled off,' Luke promised. 'I was wondering where you'd got to, and our invalid insisted I come check on you before he would take a nap.'

'How's he doing?'

'Pretty good. He ate all his lunch, and I've given him the next dose of painkillers. Thankfully he only had one small broken bone in his wrist, so the doctor was able to give him a muscle relaxant and manipulate it back into place before immobilizing it in a splint.' Suddenly he bent down and sniffed her hair. 'You might want to shower before you do anything else. It smells as though you've chain-smoked your way through a couple packs of cigarettes.'

Overwhelmed by embarrassment, tiredness and a general feeling of uselessness, Gill's eyes filled with tears. Hopelessly, she tried to brush them away, but they trickled down her cheeks.

'Oh, heck, don't cry,' Luke pleaded. 'I can cope with anything but that.'

Through her sobs Gill almost smiled. She'd found the man's Achilles heel. Next thing she knew, he wrapped his arms around her and was patting gently on her back while he murmured soothing words she guessed were supposed to make her feel better. The words themselves didn't register, but his solid warmth and caring did the trick. She rested her head against his thick flannel shirt and wanted nothing more than to stay there a very long time.

'Do either of you work here?'

A woman's harsh, demanding voice rang out behind them, and Gill pushed away from Luke before turning around. She quickly plastered on what she hoped was a welcoming smile, but the tall, angular stranger dressed all in fashionable black and running her disdainful gaze over them clearly wasn't impressed.

Gill wished the ground would open up under her.

8

'I did ring the bell,' the woman declared imperiously.

'I'm very sorry,' Gill hurried to apologize. She was here to help keep her aunt's business afloat, not almost destroy her kitchen and flirt with the handyman. 'I'm afraid we don't have any vacancies. If you're looking — '

'We supposedly have two rooms reserved. I'm Portia Silverman; and my boyfriend, Harry Warburton, is bringing our bags in from the taxi.'

Before Gill could think of a reply, Luke gave her arm a gentle squeeze, then flashed one of his most charming smiles at the new arrival. 'Welcome to the Long River Inn. I'm Luke Sawyer and this is Gillian Robinson. There must have been a slight hitch in the arrangements, as we didn't expect the pleasure of your company until tomorrow, but it's not a problem,' he said smoothly, and the woman's hollow cheeks took on a hint of colour.

'I do believe we might have said that originally, but Harry was concerned about the weather and thought we should get here early,' she conceded with a brief, tight smile.

'How about we bring a tray of coffee out to the lobby, and you can relax while we put the finishing touches to your rooms?' Luke suggested.

'That would work.'

'Is Miss Helen Monkton travelling with you?' he asked, and Gill wished she'd also been smart enough to do some homework on their expected guests.

Portia's face hardened. 'No,' she snapped, and Gill caught a twitch in Luke's mouth as though he were stifling a laugh. 'Please don't tell me she's staying here, too?'

'Yes. Mockingbird Farm booked y'all in when they ran out of rooms,' Luke explained. 'We've put you and Mr

Warburton in two of our upstairs rooms, and Miss Monkton will be downstairs.'

Gill guessed he'd just decided all that in his head, but couldn't object, as she didn't have a clue what was going on. She stood to one side while Luke shepherded their new guest out of the kitchen, at a complete loss about what to do first.

'Right, we don't have time to make proper coffee, so they'll have to make do with instant,' Luke returned. 'I'll apologize and promise them the real thing later. They already think we're hicks, so it'll just give them something else to grouse about.'

She gave up the pretence of being in charge. 'What do you want me to do?'

'Hurry up to Mr Walton's room. Strip the bed and remake it. Give the bathroom a quick clean and hang fresh towels. Then pack up all his stuff and put it in the store cupboard for now. I'll bring it down for him later. You can check on the Helena Suite, but it should be ready.' He rattled off the instructions while he put water on to boil and started to get another tray laid for the coffee.

'Out of interest, why doesn't my aunt use the other upstairs rooms?' She'd noticed several locked doors when she was looking around earlier.

'They used to have two more up and running when Hank was still around. It's too much for her to manage now, although maybe if I . . . ' Luke let the conversation drift to a close by turning his back on her to see to the coffee.

'I'll leave you to it, and thanks again,' Gill said with a smile.

'What for?' he asked, giving her a curious look over his shoulder.

'I haven't got time to list it all now.' She walked away. That should give him something to think about.

* * *

Portia Silverman swept down the stairs in a waft of expensive perfume, looking extremely glamorous in a black satin sheath and impossibly high shoes. Gill glanced up from laying the table ready for tomorrow's breakfast and mentally stamped on the surge of envy shooting through her. On her meagre salary she could only drool over designer fashions in glossy magazines, but even she recognized quality when she saw it.

'The car is here from Mockingbird Farms whenever you're ready,' she informed her guest. They were off to a pre-wedding cocktail party with the rest of the early arrivals, which let her off having to produce dessert tonight, as they wouldn't be back until late.

'Harry is on his way.' Portia tossed a gauzy silver pashmina around her bare shoulders and sighed. 'This is going to be so tedious.'

Gill couldn't imagine why any woman would hate being dressed in wonderful clothes and going off to a classy party in an upscale resort. She'd love someone to give her the chance.

'Come on, Harry, let's get this over

with,' Portia complained to the man now walking down the stairs, equally well-dressed in an immaculate black Italian suit and open-necked white silk shirt. He was easy on the eye, Gill decided, and in his manners as well. He'd been very polite earlier — nothing like his companion — and she'd immediately taken to him.

'Don't be such a grouch. You know you love Marti and Johnny to death.' He seized Portia's hand and eyed her up and down. 'Very nice. You'll be the smartest woman there, and you know it.' He gave her a laconic smile, which made her simper like a teenage girl. Over his shoulder he caught Gill's eye and winked.

Gill quickly turned away and pretended to straighten the cutlery. As the couple headed towards the door, she glanced back up to wish them a pleasant evening, and noticed Luke leaning against the kitchen door with his sharp green-eyed gaze fixed on her. She managed to go through the motions, and as her guests left she walked over to close the door behind them.

'Feeling like Cinderella, are we?' he teased and strolled across, dropping down into the nearest comfortable chair and stretching his long denim-clad legs out in front of him.

'Certainly not. You do have a vivid imagination,' Gill replied as politely as she could manage. 'How is Mr Walton doing?'

A wry smile tugged at Luke's mouth. He knew she was being purposely obtuse. 'Not too bad. Would I be right in guessing you haven't thought about dinner?'

'Not really. I imagined I could make do with a tin of soup.' She could do with some quiet time, and the idea of a peaceful evening alone in Betsy's cottage was very appealing.

'That's totally up to you, but I thought as Mr Walton is stuck here, the least we can do is feed him,' he commented.

That hadn't occurred to her, and she could have kicked herself for being so thoughtless. Whatever was wrong with her?

'Hey, don't beat yourself up. It's one of your favourite occupations, isn't it?'

Luke's shrewd comment hit home and Gill was struck dumb. She didn't get how a man she barely knew saw through her far more clearly than Michael ever did. If Michael was in a bad mood or didn't enjoy a film they went to see, she'd always blamed herself, and he'd been happy to let her.

'If it's good with you, I'll call for pizza and fix us a salad to go with it,' Luke offered.

She managed to nod, and he didn't appear bothered by her silence. 'I'll put a few more logs on the fire and help Mr Walton to come out here for a change from his room.' He got up and went over to crouch down at the fireplace, adding more wood and poking it gently to encourage the warmth out into the room. 'Anything you don't like on your pizza?' he asked as he straightened back to standing.

'I'm not a fan of anchovies or olives,' Gill ventured.

'Heathen woman.' Luke sighed, and before she could say she'd eat them if they were there, he laughed and pointed a finger at her. 'Caught you again. They're on my hate list, too.' He took out his phone and quickly called and placed an order. 'It'll be about a half hour. I'll bring Thaddeus out so you can chat while I get the salads made.'

'I could manage all that. Didn't you have any other plans for your evening? Surely Aunt Betsy doesn't have you working twenty-four hours a day.' The question tumbled out, and Luke's face turned hard as stone.

'I can *never* do enough to repay her, all right?' Without another word he stalked off, leaving her open-mouthed.

She didn't have a clue what that was about, but would get to the bottom of it before she left if it killed her. There was no way to ask him outright without having her head bitten off, so she'd have to be clever. Mr Walton might be her best bet because he'd stayed at the inn many times and obviously knew Luke well. The question was whether she could persuade him to open up to her.

She moved to sit closer to the fire and curled her feet up under her on the sofa. With all that had been going on, she'd almost forgotten tomorrow was Christmas Eve. A wave of sadness swept over her and she swallowed it back down.

'Missing home, my dear?' Mr Walton's kind voice next to her interrupted her musing, and she turned to smile at him, mentally shaking herself.

'A little.' Better that he thought she was homesick rather than moping over a cancelled wedding and messed-up life. 'But it's wonderful to be here, so I'm not complaining.' She patted the seat next to her. 'Come and join me. We can be lazy together while Luke gets

dinner organized. How are you feeling?'
She held out a hand to help him, but
the older man ignored her and lowered
himself gingerly onto the sofa and got
settled.

'Much better for taking a nice long
nap. And do let me thank you for
suggesting I stay a few extra days.' He
brushed away her attempt to dismiss his
thanks. 'Luke was kind enough to imply
I'd be doing you a favour by staying at
a reduced rate to 'keep the room
warm', as he put it. We both know it's
a fabrication, but I appreciated his
diplomacy.'

Gill tried very hard to resist probing
but her natural curiosity wouldn't rest.
'He's been kind to me, too. Very
helpful.'

'He would be. Your dear aunt would
never forgive him otherwise,' he replied
with a decided twinkle in his eye.

'You've known him a long time?'

Mr Walton reached over and covered
her hand with his own. 'Long enough to
know he's an honourable man, and I

don't say that lightly.'

In the nicest possible way Gill knew she'd been reprimanded, but couldn't blame him. She had no right to question Luke or his motives on anything. She was here for a couple of weeks to help out, nothing more and nothing less. 'I understand, and thank you.' He didn't ask her what for, and they sat comfortably together without speaking, enjoying the quiet and warmth.

Luke suddenly appeared by Gill's side, bearing a loaded tray. 'Here we go, ladies and gentlemen.'

She met his disingenuous smile, but it betrayed nothing, and she couldn't help wondering how long he'd been standing there and how much he might have heard.

9

Gill struggled to hide her yawn, swiftly covering her mouth with her hand.

'I'll hang around here to lock up after they get back. You go on to bed. You're worn out,' Luke declared. She really wanted to protest, but her brain was too tired to put together a valid argument. 'It's not a problem. I already told Mr Walton to call me in the night if he needs any help, because I figured he might rather ask me.'

'Oh, I hadn't thought about that.' He really was a considerate man, but she wasn't stupid enough to say so and embarrass them both. 'If you're sure?' she attempted as a token protest, but he only laughed and grabbed hold of her arms.

'I am. Now go and get some sleep. Do you want me to get a couple of things out of the freezer for breakfast?'

It hadn't occurred to her. He must think she had the brain of a cotton-wool ball. 'That'd be great.' She picked up her cardigan and headed across the room. 'Luke, before my aunt got sick, did you have other plans for the holidays?'

'No.' He hesitated. 'I have nowhere else to go,' he murmured, glancing briefly down at his feet before lifting his head and defiantly meeting her appalled stare. The sadness of his words took her breath away, and for several long moments neither of them spoke. 'Good night, Gill.' His dark eyes pleaded with her not to ask any more questions and she nodded, walking away while she still could.

Gill understood all about not wanting people to pry. She had very carefully skirted around Mr Walton's questions about her family and life in England earlier. Once she got through Christmas Eve tomorrow, she would feel as though a line had been drawn under the whole episode. When her mother had gently asked whether she might want to look for a new job, Gill bit her head off. It'd seemed like giving in and being a coward, but now she wondered if she were being unnecessarily hard on herself. Why was she putting herself through the aggravation when there was no need? She could look for another teaching job, or even consider trying something new. It was something to consider while she was here.

She pushed open the heavy door to step outside and shivered as the icy wind cut through her. It had got a lot colder over the last few hours, and she pulled her cardigan in around her as she hurried along the path. At the cottage she turned the key in the door and noticed tonight's clear, starry sky. She wondered how Aunt Betsy was getting on in Florida, and hoped the warmth there was doing her good. Maybe on Christmas Day she'd ring her up for a chat and tell her how things were going.

She went around turning on the lights and the small electric fire her aunt had in the small living room to supplement the central heating. With the kettle turned on to boil, she changed into her pink flannel pyjamas and matching fluffy slippers. Finally, she felt cosy and relaxed for the first time all day. She returned to the kitchen and made herself a large mug of cocoa before stretching out on the sofa.

Her eyes were drawn to the photo album on the coffee table, and she couldn't resist picking it up. She opened it to the first page and smiled at wedding photos of her aunt and uncle. At only eighteen Betsy had been a pretty girl, gazing adoringly at her handsome young husband in his smart military uniform. *You don't look as though you have any doubts*, she thought, *and yet you can't have known where your life together would lead you.*

She carried on turning the pages and followed them on their travels from England to a base in Germany, and then over to California and Texas.

Finally she discovered the first pictures of them at the inn taken back in nineteen eighty-nine. She hadn't appreciated until now how rundown the place was when they took over. It must have taken an incredible amount of work to get the inn looking as amazing as it did today.

A loud rattling noise startled her and she set down the album. Someone was banging on the door but she froze, unable to move.

'Gill, it's Luke.'

She relaxed at the sound of his voice. Goodness knew who or what she'd thought was out there. 'Coming.' Tossing off the blanket she'd been wrapped up in, she ran over and threw open the door. 'Hurry up and get inside before we both freeze to death.'

'Yes, ma'am,' he teased and stepped in, closing the door behind him. 'I have to say I'm not sure there's much chance of you getting cold in all that gear.' She met his amused eyes as they checked out her unfashionable ensemble and a fierce, hot blush lit up her skin.

'I like to be comfortable. I'm not Portia Silverman.'

'Thank the Lord,' Luke pronounced with a decided air of relief. 'The inn couldn't take two divas.'

Gill wasn't sure what he meant by that. Being logical, she knew she wasn't the type of woman to excite intrigue where men were concerned, but sometimes wondered what it must be like to have that sort of effect.

Luke smacked his head. 'You've distracted me. At least, the bunny slippers have. I'm forgetting why I came over in the first place.'

'I understand bunny slippers can do that to a man,' she teased, and then quickly pressed her lips shut. Flirting was not on her agenda. How many times would she have to keep telling herself that where this man was concerned?

'They certainly can, honey,' he drawled, and Gill wilted under the power of another of his thousand-watt smiles. He dispensed them sparingly, but when she was on the receiving end of one she couldn't resist.

'So why are you here?' Stumbling over her words, she realized how rude she'd sounded and tried to backtrack. 'Sorry, I didn't mean — '

'Your mother called. She'd tried your cell phone but it wasn't turned on, so she called the main number for the inn. I would've transferred her, but thought you might be in the bath or something and didn't want her to miss you. She's going to try again in a few minutes.'

'Did she say anything was wrong? Only, it's very late there — or early, depending on which way you look at it.' Gill frowned.

'No.' He reached out and touched her cheek, stroking his fingers gently over her heated skin. 'You're a real worrier, aren't you? I got the impression she'd received your emails but wanted to hear your voice, that's all.' She stepped backwards and he grabbed her arm, stopping her falling over the table. 'Hey, I'm sorry. I didn't mean to . . . '

He dropped his hands back to his sides.

'No, I'm the one who's sorry. I — '

The phone jangled to life and neither of them moved.

'Answer it. I'll go,' Luke insisted, heading for the door before she could protest.

Gill turned away and snatched up the phone. 'Mum?' The wonderful sound of her mother's voice made her forget everything else, and she curled back up on the sofa to enjoy a good long chat.

'How are things? Are you managing all right?' her mother asked, and Gill wondered how honestly to reply. She decided a little creativity wouldn't be a bad idea.

'Pretty good. The inn is bigger than I'd imagined, and there's a bit more involved to the cooking than I'd anticipated.' *Understatement.* 'Luckily the handyman who works here knows a lot about the running of the place, and he's been very helpful.' Gill deliberately left out the fact she found Luke Sawyer extremely tempting, because she didn't intend to act on her weakness, plus she didn't need her mother to worry.

'That's nice to hear.' Patricia hesitated. 'And what about you?'

'What about me — ?' Gill wasn't stupid. She knew what her mother was getting at, but didn't want her thinking it was foremost in her mind.

'How are you doing? You know with tomorrow being, well, Christmas Eve. I couldn't sleep for thinking about you.'

Gill took a long, deep breath and slowly exhaled before answering. 'I'm honestly okay.' Strangely enough, she meant it. Apart from her brief glitch earlier this evening, she hadn't given Michael and the cancelled wedding much thought at all. 'I've been too busy to brood. I'm glad you encouraged me to come.'

'Oh, that's such a relief. I was worried I shouldn't have pushed you.' Her mother chattered on and Gill let her ramble for a few more minutes.

'You need to get some sleep or it'll be time for you to get up again soon,' Gill teased. 'I'm going to have an early night and get ready for a busy few days. How about we talk again on Christmas Day when Brian and his family are all there?'

They made their plans and said good night. After Gill hung up the phone, she couldn't help thinking about Luke again, and her overreaction when he'd touched her. He'd got the impression he'd offended her, and maybe it was better he carried on believing that for both their sakes.

She picked the photo album back up and turned to the next page. Her heart leapt into her throat as she stared at the picture in front of her.

10

The date on the photo was New Year's Eve fifteen years ago, and it had obviously been taken on the front porch of the inn. Her smiling aunt and uncle stood in the centre, while a crowd of people gathered around them in the background, holding up their glasses and toasting the New Year.

It was the sight of the thin, frowning teenage boy sandwiched awkwardly between Betsy and Hank that had startled her. Despite the shaggy hair and dark-rimmed glasses, Gill recognized Luke in an instant. His unusual eyes stood out, and even then he'd had the same air of separateness.

None of this made sense, but the idea of asking Luke about it outright made Gill uneasy. It wasn't as if he'd lied to her; he'd just never mentioned how long he'd lived here. Her assumption that he'd simply been employed as a handyman when her aunt and uncle needed help was plainly false.

She carried on looking through the album and found several more pictures of Luke. The one that interested her most was taken in a cap and gown and was obviously a university graduation celebration. He towered over Betsy and Hank and had his arms around their shoulders, with all three of them smiling broadly into the camera.

I can never do enough to repay her, all right? Luke's words snaked back into her brain and began to make more sense.

She glanced at the clock and realized she should be getting to bed in order to face Christmas Eve tomorrow. She rather thought she'd keep the finding of these photos to herself for now.

★　★　★

Gill had purposely set her alarm early, determined not to get behind before the day even started. She selected a new pair of slim, dark jeans and a soft red scoop-neck jumper, and got dressed before popping on her scarlet leather flats so her feet wouldn't get tired with standing more than usual. In the middle of doing her makeup, she stopped with the mascara wand in her hand as an unexpected wave of sadness swept over her. *So much for being okay.*

The images rolled unbidden through her head in a continuous loop. The Vera Wang knockoff gown. Dark green brides-maids' dresses. Red roses in extravagant hand-tied bouquets. A carriage drawn by white horses. A winter wonderland-themed reception.

You've always been more in love with the idea of being married than me. When you can admit that, you'll be a lot happier . . . He was both right and wrong, and Gill could see that now. Right in the sense she did love the idea of marriage, but that was because she'd seen how wonderful it could be and craved that for herself. She didn't see any shame in that. But where he'd been wrong was in thinking she hadn't loved him. She truly had as a sixteen-year-old starry-eyed teenager; but they'd both changed, and their love hadn't matured along with them, leaving her stuck with her old dreams.

It was time to create new ones, but she didn't know where to start.

Her elbow slipped off the edge of the dresser and she poked the mascara wand in her eye. 'Drat,' she mumbled, rubbing at her sore eye. Peering in the mirror, she stared aghast at the black smeary mess she'd made. Now she'd have to remove it all and start again. The clock beeped with its final time-to-get-going call and she groaned. Seven o'clock already. She wanted to get everything organized for breakfast and be calm and in control by the time Luke appeared. As quickly as possible she repaired the damage and put on a slick of glossy red lipstick in an effort to look more Christmassy. Then she grabbed her puffy silver jacket from the peg by the door and tossed it on as she ran outside.

'Oh!' She ran straight into Luke's broad chest and almost fell over.

'I always have a problem with women throwing themselves at me — just didn't think you'd be one of them,' he joked, and clasped her around the waist to hold her steady.

'Don't flatter yourself,' she retorted, and pulled away. 'What do you want? I'm in a hurry.' He always wrong-footed her and made her come across as ungrateful and miserable.

'I came to see where you were, that's all,' he said with an easy smile. 'Didn't want us to be caught out by our demanding guest. Of course, she didn't get in until nearly one this morning, so may not even be down anytime soon. No doubt she only eats the equivalent of a lettuce leaf for breakfast anyway.'

Gill couldn't help smiling. The idea of the super-glamorous Portia tucking into a large plate of food was pretty absurd. 'Hot water and lemon is my guess. Maybe a slice of thin dry toast, seeing it's Christmas,' she ventured, and started to walk along the path. Luke fell into step beside her.

'Oh, come on, kid. I bet she'll throw caution to the winds and have an egg-white omelette as her once-a-year treat.' Luke's friendly banter eased the knot of tension lurking at the base of Gill's stomach. 'Don't think I'm usurping my authority, but I've turned the oven on for you and put the coffee on.'

Part of her wanted to tell him off, but the honest side of her couldn't. He'd saved her again, and it wasn't his fault she resented it. 'Thank you.'

'You're welcome. I checked on Thaddeus and he's doing fine. I said I'll bring him in a tray so he doesn't have to bother dressing yet.' He flashed a broad grin. 'Not sure he could stomach our sharp-tongued lady first thing in the morning.'

'Can any of us?' Gill rolled her eyes.

Luke stepped forward to open the

door, letting her go in first. 'Trust me, I'll happily leave you to serve breakfast while I find something useful to do out of the way.'

She hoped he wouldn't totally abandon her but couldn't say so without sounding a complete wimp. 'I'm sure you can find something to fix.'

'Oh, I'm sure I can, sweetheart.' His gaze lingered on her a little too long to be polite and Gill felt a rush of heat flame her cheeks. Outside the kitchen door he stopped and lightly touched her arm. 'Anything I can do other than leave you alone?'

'I think I'll be fine. I should have it all ready on time.' Mentally she crossed her fingers and toes that for once she could get things together without Luke's help. 'I'll see you when you come to get fed.'

'I'll be with Thaddeus if you need me.' He tipped a finger to his forehead and strolled off.

Gill braced herself and pushed open the swing door. She'd come to the conclusion she must treat this the same way as a lesson at school by making a plan to get the work done in the allotted time. She quickly checked Aunt Betsy's recipe book and immediately put the western omelette casserole in the oven to warm through. Getting out a large saucepan, she tipped in the defrosted winter fruit compote and turned the heat on low. Luke had suggested wheat toast, butter and homemade peach jam alongside those dishes, so she started to get that organized. She hummed away to herself, beginning to think this wasn't so bad after all.

Harry Warburton breezed into the room, his friendly smile cheering her even more. 'Good morning, lovely lady. I know it's early, but I'm gasping for coffee. A few too many champagne cocktails last night.' He rubbed at his forehead, pushing back a lock of thick blond hair and giving her a fake ashamed smile.

'It's not a problem. I'll bring you out a tray,' she assured him, but he simply pulled out one of the stools, slid it close to her and sat, grinning like a naughty little boy.

'Ah, but then I wouldn't have the pleasure of your company. Just fix me a mug and I can adore you from here.' He gave her a long, slow wink and Gill knew she blushed horribly.

She walked over to the coffee machine and tried to steady her hands as she poured two mugs, the other a much-needed one for herself. 'There you go.' She placed his in front of him and went to check on the oven, not because anything would be ready yet, but to put some distance between herself and him. He was a nice man, but she wasn't interested in *that* way, and didn't want him to get the wrong impression. 'I hope you enjoyed your party last night?' she asked him.

'Sure did. Portia's going to some ladies' lunch thing today and leaving me all alone. Some of the guys are going on a hike, but that's not really my thing. How about you take pity on me and we go explore the local area together?' he pleaded.

'Thank you for the invitation, but I have a lot of work to do here,' Gill explained. It was the absolute truth, considering on top of everything else she'd given no thought to what they were going to eat for Christmas dinner tomorrow. The wedding guests should be tied up with the continuing festivities, but Mr Walton and Luke would be around. She'd never cooked a turkey in her life, mainly because her mum always shooed her out of the kitchen and she never objected. Gill didn't have a clue what people here even ate for Christmas.

'All work and no play makes Gill a dull girl,' Harry teased, getting up to wander across and stand right in front of her. If she stepped backwards she'd be up against the hot oven, and one step forward and she'd crash right into his chest. A slow touch of amusement crept across his face. 'Oh, look what I've found.' He pulled something out of his pocket and waved it above her head. Gill craned her neck to see him holding a large sprig of mistletoe in his fingers. He stared right down into her and his bright blue eyes sparkled with mischief. 'Merry Christmas.'

Gill flinched as his warm lips pressed against her mouth.

'Is breakfast ready?' Luke's deep voice startled her and she pulled away from Harry's embrace. 'Excuse me. I didn't mean to interrupt.' His icy tone cut right through her.

'You weren't,' she protested. 'We were just — '

'No explanation needed,' he cut her off, and stalked from the room.

Harry smirked and waved the mistletoe around. 'Now, where were we?'

'You were leaving. I'm fixing breakfast.' Gill managed a tight smile and shooed him off.

11

Gill slumped against the counter and slowly counted to ten. What must Luke think of her? *Why do I care?* She wasn't about to answer *that* question. An insistent beeping noise interrupted her thoughts and she realized it was coming from her watch. She'd set the alarm to remind her about taking the casserole out of the oven because Luke hadn't fixed the timer yet. Before she could have another culinary disaster, she grabbed the oven mitts and opened the door, pulling out the golden-brown bubbling dish with a satisfied smile.

She set the casserole on the counter to cool, then checked on the fruit compote. She gave it a good stir and then tipped it into the serving dish ready to take into the other room. So far, so good. She didn't want to make the toast until her guests were ready, so she headed out to check if they'd arrived.

'I'm waiting patiently as instructed, lovely lady,' Harry joked, sipping at his coffee.

Gill put on her best professional smile. 'Will Ms Silverman be joining you for breakfast?'

'Shouldn't think so, sweetheart. All she did was groan under the covers when I checked on her earlier. Solid food rarely passes her lips before noon,' he explained, and she wished he hadn't mentioned the word 'lips' to bring back uncomfortable memories of their kitchen fiasco.

'I'll go ahead and serve you.' She made her escape before he could embarrass her any more. She started to get everything ready, and while she was stacking toast on a plate the door swung open and Luke walked in, unsmiling and silent.

'I'll help you take all this in and dish up a couple of plates to take to Thaddeus's room.'

His curt words annoyed her. Who did he think he was? She pulled herself up to her full five feet five and a half inches and stared him in the face. 'Don't you think you're overreacting?'

'To what?' He sounded genuinely confused, but she wasn't about to let him get away with it. She was a free woman. The fact that she hadn't sought Harry Warburton's kiss and didn't have the slightest interest in him was irrelevant.

'It's Christmas, if you hadn't noticed, and Harry is a man who likes to flirt. It wasn't a big deal,' Gill tried to explain, while still mad at herself for even feeling the need to. 'Haven't you ever kissed a woman under the mistletoe just because?'

Luke stepped closer and she felt the heat emanating from his body. 'If *I* kissed you it *would* be a big deal.' His deep raspy voice tightened something deep in her gut and she struggled to speak.

'Really?' she whispered, running her

fingers up over his dark green flannel shirt to linger on his broad chest.

He slid one hand back behind her neck to cup her head, bringing it closer to his mouth. Gill's heart raced and his lips brushed hers, so lightly it was barely a touch, but it was enough to set her on fire.

'Do you have any . . . Good grief, do you two spend all your time pawing each other in here?' Portia's disgusted voice filled the room.

Gill sighed and reluctantly let go of Luke before managing a fake bright smile. 'We do try not to,' she said sweetly, and Luke covered up a choking sound with a loud cough. 'We were about to bring breakfast out.'

Portia's sharp eyed gaze swept over the assembled food and she exhaled a loud sigh. 'I came in to ask if you had any herbal teas, but now I'm looking at this selection of food I do hope there's something else on offer.' She ran her hands down over her tight-fitting red dress. 'You may have given up on your figure, but I haven't.'

Gill bit her tongue at the scathing assessment of her appearance and didn't dare risk looking at Luke.

'I'd prefer to still fit into my clothes and not suffer blocked arteries and a fatal stroke after eating breakfast.' Portia stared at the offending casserole as if it contained a hefty dose of arsenic. 'I was thinking more along the lines of an egg-white omelette with a little spinach and tomato, and maybe some fresh fruit.'

Now Gill really did have to stifle every last humour cell in her body at the mention of the very dish Luke had guessed Portia might request. 'I'm sure we can arrange that for you. It's not a problem.' Actually it was, because she'd never cooked an omelette in her life, but she hoped the super-efficient man still glued to her side would come through again. 'I'll bring hot water and a selection of teabags in for you.' Thank goodness she knew they did have those.

'Oh, and I almost forgot to mention,

your other wedding guest has arrived,' Portia said, a distasteful look marring her elegant face.

'Already?'

'The stupid girl talked her doting father into sending her in a limo all the way from New York,' Portia mocked, and Gill's enthusiasm for the day declined even further. Another demanding guest was exactly what she didn't need. 'The ladies are having a bridal lunch, so you'll be stuck amusing Harry. We'll be back here by three to get ready for the ceremony, which is at six. Naturally, the party will go on well into the night afterwards, so I assume someone will be here to lock up after us later?'

'Of course,' Luke jumped in. 'I'll be waiting.'

The arrogant woman nodded with no hint of thanks for the inconvenience. 'Tomorrow we'll be attending the farewell brunch before leaving, so you won't have to worry about providing a Christmas meal for us,' Portia added, as though she were doing them a favour. Gill stopped herself from saying that they were only a bed and breakfast after all. She was being let off the hook for evening dessert again, apart from the three of them, and she guessed Luke and Thaddeus would be easy to please.

'You might make sure you take warm coats and boots with you tonight,' Luke spoke up. 'The bad weather may be here as early as tomorrow morning. I'll check the forecast again later and let you know what's in store when you get back from the wedding so you can adjust your travel plans accordingly.'

'Mockingbird Farm will provide anything we need and take good care of us; they prepare everything for their guests and have been most solicitous because of us having to be placed in inferior accommodation,' Portia responded snidely, and Gill had an overwhelming urge to smack her self-satisfied face.

'Time for breakfast, I think,' Gill declared, and Luke took the hint and went to fetch the coffee pot. She allowed Portia to go first and followed her out with the tray of food. Near the table she stopped and stared at the young woman whose arms were draped around Harry's neck.

'Hey, big sister, is that breakfast? I'm starving,' she laughed over at them.

Sister? Why hadn't Portia mentioned the fact they were related?

Portia turned to Gill with a sigh. 'Ms Anderson, this is Helen Monkton, my half-sister.' The emphasis on the word 'half' was chilling, and plainly there was no love lost on Portia's side of the equation. 'I'm sure *she'll* eat whatever you put out. She isn't fussy.' The put-down didn't seem to bother the younger woman, who riffled her hands through Harry's hair and giggled.

'Oh, Porky, stop it. These poor people will think you don't like me,' Helen said with a pout.

'For goodness sake, don't call me by that stupid name. You're not five years old anymore,' Portia snapped, and pulled out a chair to sit down. She glared at Gill. 'Is there any chance we might get breakfast sometime today?'

Gill managed a tight smile. 'Of course.' She arranged the dishes on the table and prepared to go back to the kitchen. 'Your omelette will be ready soon.' After she tossed a pleading glance at Luke, he followed her out.

'Need a little rescuing, do we?' he teased, and she had to swallow her pride and nod. 'Thought you might. I took a couple of eggs out of the fridge to come to room temperature.'

'Why?'

'They beat up to a greater volume and will make an omelette to impress even the picky Miss Porky,' he declared.

Gill giggled. 'Wasn't that the funniest thing? I thought she'd kill her sister on the spot.'

'Your aunt hasn't lost a guest yet, so let's try not to break her winning streak.' His dry declaration was accompanied by one of his irresistible smiles. 'You can fix a plate of fresh fruit. It shouldn't challenge your culinary skills too much.'

'Fine.' She tried to sound put out,

but didn't put her heart into it and was rewarded by a swift kiss on her forehead. 'Oh.'

'Good girl. You didn't argue for once.' He patted her backside as he strolled over to the oven, whistling a cheerful tune as he went.

Gill wanted to be outraged, she really did. So why was she smiling like a lovesick teenager?

12

Determined to ignore him, Gill took out a small selection of strawberries, melon chunks, and grapes from the fridge. She took her time arranging them prettily on one of her aunt's antique tea plates while out of the corner of her eye she observed Luke. First he heated olive oil in a small frying pan, before adding spinach and chopped tomatoes and stirring for a while. He tasted the mixture and added salt and pepper before putting that to one side. Turning back to the counter, he started on the eggs. Deftly he separated them and started to beat the whites with a whisk, adding a touch of water.

'Are you ready for the impressive bit?' He smiled back over his shoulder at her and she gave up pretending not to watch. He had another frying pan ready and added the egg-white mixture, swirling it rapidly around before standing back. 'You've got to let it set a bit before pushing the edges in to let the uncooked mixture reach the heat.' He worked on it some more and then reached for the filling, adding that to one side before neatly folding the omelette over and sliding the whole thing onto a plate he'd had warming under the grill. 'Come on. It's time to face the lioness in her den.' He sauntered towards the kitchen door and Gill grabbed the fruit plate and followed.

She held her breath as Portia examined the omelette placed in front of her, then cut a small piece and stabbed it with her fork before placing it in her mouth and chewing slowly. 'Not bad,' she commented, and Gill guessed that was her idea of high praise.

'I'll fix a plate and take it to Mr Walton,' Luke said, and started to get one together.

'What about you?' Gill asked him.

He shook his head at her question. 'Later.' His eyes darkened and rested on her. 'I'll eat mine with you,' he murmured under his breath.

Gill glanced away, blushing furiously, and tried to concentrate on her guests. 'I hope you all enjoy your breakfast. I'll be in the kitchen, so just ring the bell if you need anything else.' She pointed to the silver bell and quickly made her escape. Closing the door behind her with relief, she began to clean up.

A mass of conflicting thoughts jostled around her mind. She'd expected to be sad and moping all day, but instead she was full of energy and tingling from Luke's brief kiss. She couldn't decide if this was good or not. There wasn't much else she could do until her guests finished breakfast, so she put the kettle on to boil to make herself some tea.

'Isn't that the British cure for everything?' Luke said with a laugh as he came in. He walked over to the sink and set down the dirty breakfast dishes he was carrying. 'Is there enough for two in the pot?'

'You drink tea?' she asked.

'Of course. Betsy trained me well over the years.'

Gill hesitated for a second. He was the one who'd mentioned it, so what could be the harm in an innocent question? 'Have you lived here long?'

Luke didn't answer straight away. He rinsed off the plates and loaded everything into the dishwasher before turning back around to face her. 'Why ask when you know the answer?' He barely spoke loud enough for her to hear, the tight line of his jaw the only sign of his tension. 'I'm not stupid, Gill, so don't treat me as if I am. We both know you were looking at Betsy's photo album last night.'

It took all her strength to meet his scathing eyes. 'So? Is it a big secret?' she asked as calmly as she could manage.

He took his time and walked back across to stop in front of her, his nearness making her heart thump.

Without speaking, he selected a mug and poured in a small amount of milk before adding the tea. 'My past isn't much to brag about.'

Gill reached out to rest her hand on top of his on the counter. 'I didn't mean to offend you. I'm sorry. Forget it.'

'Easier said than done, isn't it?' A thread of sadness ran through his voice and she wished she'd kept her mouth shut. 'I've never talked about it to anyone. I didn't even tell Betsy and Hank the whole story.'

'I don't expect — '

Luke leaned over and silenced her with a soft kiss. 'I want to share it with you, but not today. When everyone's gone and we're here alone, I might be able to then. Are you good with that for now?' He frowned, and she ached to brush away the worry etched on his face. The words *when everyone's gone and we're here alone* sank in and she swallowed hard. She wondered what would happen with no guests as a

117

buffer between them.

'Yes.' She smiled. 'Now, how about breakfast?'

'You sure know how to win a starving guy over, sweetheart,' he responded, playing along with her effort to get them back on safer ground. 'Why don't you sit still and I'll get the dishes in from the other room, see what's left and fix us a couple of plates.'

Gill could have protested but decided it would be foolish. Instead she simply thanked him and was rewarded by one of his heart-warming smiles. He didn't take long; his quiet efficiency always impressed her because nothing seemed to be a big deal for him. Soon they were eating, and she sighed with happiness as she dug into the leftover casserole and warm, spicy fruit. He'd made them fresh toast and set out the local butter and homemade jam as well.

'Did you enjoy that?' he asked in his soft, teasing drawl when she laid down her knife and fork on the empty plate.

'No, it was terrible. I was being very

polite and British,' she tossed back at him, and he burst out laughing.

'Thought so. I believe we'll let you cook our Christmas dinner tomorrow so you can show us how it's done,' he said with such a serious tone to his voice she almost fell for it, until she caught the amused twinkle in his emerald eyes. 'Don't worry. I'm not into having my turkey either raw or cremated.'

Gill shrugged. 'I've never cooked one. Wouldn't know where to start.' If she wanted more honesty between them, she'd better step up herself. 'I'm happy to be your assistant. I'd been wondering what we were going to have for ourselves and Mr Walton.'

Luke launched into a long explanation about discussing it with Thaddeus and all the foods they both wanted to eat. Some sounded bizarre to her — sweet potatoes, a thing they called dressing that sounded rather like stuffing, and a fruit salad they ate with the turkey instead of as a pudding. Gill kept a smile on her face and merely agreed.

'Hey, here's me rambling on. What is there you can't do without on Christmas Day?' Luke asked her.

For a minute she almost said *you*, then stopped herself. That would be ridiculous and juvenile. 'We have traditional things, but as I'm here this year I want to make the most of it. I can have roast potatoes, sprouts and Christmas pudding any time, but I'd rather try all the foods you normally serve.'

A slow grin spread over his face and she was relieved to have said the right thing. 'You're on. I need to get your timer fixed first, and then I'll go outside and spread salt on the paths and steps so they hopefully won't get too slippery when the snow comes. Later I'll pop out and get all the groceries we need and we'll start cooking this afternoon.'

'We will?' Gill asked, very unsure about his plan.

'All you have to do is follow instructions.' He reached up and cradled her face in his hands, gently stroking his large thumbs down over her cheeks and sending shivers running through her. 'Can you do that, Gillian?' The dark, quiet way he dragged out her name got to her and she could only nod. 'Good.'

'I ought to finish up in here,' she said. 'I won't be able to do the women's bedrooms until they go out later. Do you think Mr Walton would mind me going in to clean his while he's there?'

Luke shook his head. 'I'm sure that'll be fine. He'll be glad to chat.' He picked up one of her hands and toyed with her fingers. 'You might want to make sure our local Casanova isn't in his room when you're ready to do his.'

She took a chance on teasing him. 'Jealous?'

'Maybe,' Luke growled. 'Are you satisfied now?'

'I do believe I am.' She jumped up and ran towards the door with an extra spring in her step, then disappeared back into the other room with Luke's laughter ringing in her ears.

'Gillian Elizabeth, you're exactly like your mother,' came a reedy voice from across the room. 'I'd bet anything you never sit still.'

Gill stopped dead in her tracks and stared at the wrinkled, grey-haired old woman in the doorway leaning heavily on a cane and surrounded by a pile of mismatched luggage.

'Aren't you going to come and give your aunty a hug?'

'Aunt Betsy?' she whispered. The slivers of overheard conversation and silenced hints she'd got from Luke and Mr Walton clicked into place. Her aunt hadn't gone to Florida simply for the warm weather. Only a few years older than her own mother, this Betsy was a shadow of the energetic woman she remembered from her last visit to Cornwall.

Gill walked forward and stepped into her aunt's outstretched arms, fighting back tears.

13

'What are you doing here?' she blurted out before realizing how rude she sounded. 'Sorry, I meant — '

Betsy smiled. 'Shush, dear, it's okay. I couldn't stand being away over Christmas after all.'

'But it's so cold here, and we're going to get snow, and I thought the doctors said you needed to be where it was warmer,' Gill rattled on, and her aunt only laughed. Suddenly her laugh turned into a harsh wracking cough, and Betsy grabbed at her arm.

'Help me to a chair, Gillian,' she gasped, struggling to breathe.

Gently she led her aunt over to the table and pulled out the closest chair before helping her to sit down. 'Would you like a glass of water?' Betsy nodded, still unable to talk, and Gill hurried over to the dresser where they always kept a fresh jug of water. Her hands shook as she selected a clean glass and filled it up. If only someone had warned her, it wouldn't have been such a shock to see the deterioration in her aunt's health. For a few seconds Gill kept her back to her aunt and took deep, slow breaths in an effort to get back in control of herself. Then she managed a bright smile and walked back across the room.

'There you are.' She put the glass into her aunt's hand. 'Is there anything else I can do?'

Betsy shook her head and sipped the water until her cough subsided. 'That's better.' She set the glass back down and Gill felt herself being studied. 'The dear boy didn't tell you, did he?'

Gill shook her head, not bothering to pretend she didn't know who or what her aunt was talking about.

'Luke's not a man to break his promises,' Betsy said with a sad smile. 'I knew he wouldn't let me down.'

'Mr Walton was concerned about you, too.'

'He's a good man. I suppose he's gone home by now?' Betsy asked.

Gill launched into the whole story of the accident and went on to describe their other guests. Soon she had her aunt laughing, and some of the awful grey strain left her face.

'You still haven't told me why you came home early. We're managing fine.' *If you don't count the fact I nearly burnt down your kitchen and have discovered I have absolutely no culinary skills.*

Her aunt's expression darkened again, and she clutched at the edge of the table. 'I couldn't spend Christmas away from here. Not my first one without Hank. Especially as it'll probably be my . . . ' Betsy's voice trailed away. 'Anyway, I'm here now, and I'm going to enjoy getting to know you better. We'll be out in the cottage together, which I'll be glad of. It's tough being out there on my own these days.'

'I'll move into the spare room so you can have your own bed back,' Gill declared, and refused to listen when her

125

aunt tried to protest. 'It's the least I can do. Now, how about I tell Luke you're here?'

'In a minute, dear.' Betsy patted her hand, her brown eyes shiny with curiosity. 'How are you two getting on?'

Gill smoothed down the hem of her shirt and worked on keeping her voice steady. 'Quite well.'

'He's a fine young man,' her aunt declared, and for one crazy second Gill wondered if they'd been the victim of some serious matchmaking. Betsy knew about her broken engagement, but surely she hadn't tried to pair them off?

'He's very capable.' Gill chose her words carefully. That could mean anything, or nothing. 'He's been more than helpful to me.'

Betsy beamed. 'I'm sure he has.'

Luke strode in from the kitchen, wagging a finger in the air. 'Talking about me again? What are you doing here, as if I didn't know?' He leaned down to give Betsy a kiss, and a slight blush coloured her hollowed-out cheeks. He pulled out a chair and sat down to join them before glancing over at Gill. She felt his silent apology running between them and hoped her quick returning smile let him know it was okay. 'I'll take your bags out to the cottage and Gill can help you unpack. I'll have the kettle boiled by the time you come back in.'

'The boy is a mind-reader.' Betsy chuckled. Before she could stand up, Luke was at her side, pulling her chair back and holding out his arm for her to grasp.

Gill blinked to get rid of the film of tears threatening to spill over. All she could think was that she was going to have to tell her mother how ill her sister was, because Patricia obviously didn't know, or she wouldn't have let Gill come here unprepared.

'Are you coming?' Luke asked and she nodded, relieved when he didn't say anything that demanded she reply, because she didn't think she could for a minute.

'I'll get a couple of these.' She

quickly snatched up two of the bags, glad to have something constructive to do.

Luke grasped the handle of her aunt's large suitcase with one hand and slipped the other through Betsy's elbow to cradle her arm. They made slow progress outside, and when they finally got inside the cottage Betsy sunk down on the sofa with obvious relief.

'Why don't we have our tea here instead?' Gill suggested. 'I'll turn the fire on and it'll soon be really cosy. You won't have to go back out in the cold air then.'

'That's a good idea,' Luke said quickly. 'You ladies have lots to catch up on. I've got work to do in the house, so I'll keep an eye on things there.'

Betsy glared at them both. 'So that's the way it's going to be — with the pair of you ganging up on me all the time?'

'I thought it would — ' Gill tried to protest, but Luke cut her off and wagged his finger at Betsy.

'You're a naughty woman. You were

told to go away for your health and you've stubbornly come back anyway. Now you'll have to put up with us fussing over you. It's your own fault,' he declared firmly. 'Do what you're told or I won't let you come in the house for dinner tonight.'

'But it's Christmas Eve, and we always — '

His fierce glare shut Betsy up in an instant. 'I know what you always do, but you won't if you don't rest now. After she's had tea with you, Gill can come back in to see to the bedrooms while I go to the grocery store. And, yes, I'll remember to pick up some barbeque for lunchtime.'

Betsy looked slightly shamefaced and Gill almost laughed to see her aunt put firmly in her place. Luke clearly wasn't a man to be walked over, and she liked that. More than liked it, in fact.

'I'll call to let you know when our divas have gone off for their party.' He headed for the door and left them to it.

'Am I allowed to walk into my

bedroom, or has the lord and master forbidden that too?' Betsy groused rather half-heartedly at Gill.

'I do believe it might be allowed.' She flashed a quick smile. 'I'll put the kettle on then come and help you unpack.' She hurried off and soon had a tea tray put together, which she carried back into the living room; but her aunt was nowhere to be seen, so Gill set it down on the table and went to search for her.

At the bedroom door she stopped and bit back a sigh. Her aunt was curled up on the bed, fast asleep. Gill crept across and picked up a warm plaid blanket from the chair then carefully spread it over Betsy so as not to disturb her. On the way out she quietly closed the door behind her and immediately rang Luke.

'What's up, honey?' he replied straight away.

'Nothing much, but Betsy's taking a nap and I didn't want you to phone and wake her up.'

'Come on over and I'm sure you can

find something to do, if it's only watching me work,' he joked.

'You are a very vain man,' Gill protested and hung up on him.

★ ★ ★

Ten minutes later there was no laughter between them.

'So that's it, really. It wasn't my place to tell you before.' Luke sat back and took another swig of coffee.

'Didn't Betsy think my mother had a right to know either?' Gill asked, still trying to get her head around how ill her aunt was.

He shrugged. 'Hank tried to get her to tell y'all, but she dug her heels in and refused. After he passed I watched her fall apart, but she always put on a brave face in public, so no one else appreciates how much she misses him.'

'She's lucky to have you around.' Gill took a wild guess the inn wouldn't still be up and running if it weren't for Luke.

'I won't leave while she needs me.' The fierceness in his voice was belied by his sad eyes. 'When I had nothing and no one, she took me in. That's a debt I can never repay.' He pushed back his chair and jumped up. 'One of the back windows needs a new latch.'

She watched him scurry away and wondered when she'd ever find out his full story. Maybe now she had another avenue to explore. Aunt Betsy was a woman who liked nothing better than to talk, so perhaps all Gill would need to do was encourage her.

Let him think he'd got away with distracting her again . . . for now.

14

'Well, if it isn't my favourite innkeeper.'
Harry Warburton's teasing voice coming
from somewhere behind Gill's shoulder
startled her and she dropped her duster.
As she bent down to pick it up he beat
her to it and shifted around in front
of her, waving the yellow rag in her
face.

'There you go.' He dangled it from
his fingers, yanking it away when she
tried to take it from him. 'The fine for
getting it back is one kiss. Especially
after we were interrupted last time.'

Gill folded her arms and glared.
'There are plenty more dusters where
that one came from. Also, I don't make
a habit of kissing guests.'

'I guess if I helped out in the kitchen
or could wield a hammer you might be
more amenable,' he said with a sly grin,
and Gill's smile froze in place. She

couldn't be as rude as she wanted to for her aunt's sake.

'I'm sure your mistletoe will be much appreciated at tonight's wedding,' she said lightly, and took a small step backwards.

'Harry, dear, go and see if the car is here for us,' Portia's imperious voice rang out, and for once Gill was relieved to see the other woman appear. Her guest was artfully posing on the stairs in yet another designer outfit. Today it was a beautifully cut day dress in burgundy wool, topped with a short black fur coat.

'Of course. Your wish is my command,' Harry responded; and by the taut smile on Portia's face, Gill guessed she was oblivious to the irony laced through Harry's words. She couldn't work out the true nature of their relationship, although Portia had called him her boyfriend at one point.

Helen appeared at the top of the stairs dressed in winter white and pouting quite charmingly. 'I shall feel quite left out in a minute, Harry dear.'

'Ah, the Snow Queen arrives. How is a man supposed to survive under an onslaught of such loveliness?' he quipped.

By being an incorrigible flirt. Gill kept the thought to herself and suppressed a smile as the two woman headed towards Harry.

'Stay here in the warm, ladies, while I see if your chauffeur has arrived.' He beat a hasty retreat.

'We'll be back no later than three, and expect our rooms to be cleaned by then,' Portia declared while checking out her immaculate manicure. 'We would like a selection of canapés and wine available at six before we leave for the wedding.'

Gill bit her lip. She could remind the woman this was a bed and breakfast, nothing more, but a picture of her exhausted aunt sprang to mind. She plastered on another bright smile. 'That won't be a problem.' How you made a canapé, she didn't know. Somehow she couldn't imagine that her mother's usual cheese and pineapple on sticks and cocktail sausages were what Portia had in mind.

Harry appeared at the door. 'Come on, ladies, let's get you off to the party.' He offered them each an arm and escorted them outside, returning a few moments later with a broad smile all over his face. 'Now I'm all yours.' Gill's heart sank.

Luke strolled in from the kitchen, fixing their guest with a very determined stare. 'Ah, Mr Warburton. I hear you're at a loose end?'

'Um, well, yeah.'

Gill suppressed a smile as Harry shifted his gaze between them, as if trying to work out what was going on.

'Great. Gillian has a lot to do, so she won't be able to help me spread salt outside.'

'Salt?' the other man asked, obviously puzzled.

'Yeah. We need to get the paths and steps covered before tonight. If you wouldn't mind giving me a hand, I'd be eternally grateful,' Luke said, and Gill tried not to burst out laughing.

'Of course,' Harry replied, throwing her a pleading glance, but she only smiled broadly back at him.

'Thanks. You're so kind to help us out,' she said sweetly, quickly rushing off with her duster before he could dream up another delaying tactic.

★ ★ ★

Gill managed to get the wedding guests' bedrooms finished without being pestered, and hurried towards Mr Walton's room with her cleaning supplies. She knocked before opening the door and walking in, then stopped dead at the sight of Mr Walton and her aunt sitting together on the sofa, deep in conversation.

'Oh, I'm sorry. Would you rather I went away and came back later to clean?'

'Not at all,' Thaddeus replied, patting her aunt's hand. 'We were just catching up with everything, weren't we, Betsy?' Gill had the uncomfortable feeling of being talked about.

'Oh, yes,' her aunt joined in, smiling at Gill. 'Don't let us stop you. Carry on as though we weren't here.'

'Okay.' She didn't have much choice so headed into the bathroom, purposely leaving the door open a few inches. When she'd finished a quarter of an hour later, all she had managed to overhear was them chatting about the fact the University of Tennessee football team needed to improve, and all the new varieties of tomato plants Mr Walton planned to try in his garden next summer. She went back out and walked across the room ready to make the bed.

'You're looking very pretty today, dear,' Aunt Betsy suddenly said. 'Did Luke notice?'

Gill kept her back to them and carried on straightening out the sheets. 'I can't imagine why you would think he would.'

'No particular reason.'

Gill felt the knowing looks the pair

gave each other without having to turn around. They were two elderly people with nothing better to do, and she refused to rise to their bait. She plumped up the pillows and shook out the duvet before smoothing it back into place.

'Do you want me to hoover around, or will the noise annoy you?' she asked, giving them her friendliest smile.

'I don't think it's too bad, dear,' Betsy declared. 'Why don't you run along and see if Luke has lunch ready? We'll come out there and eat with you.'

Gill kept on smiling. Wonderful. Now they'd be scrutinized all the time they ate. 'I'll pop back down when it's fixed and let you know,' she offered.

'Perfect.' Betsy sat back and patted Thaddeus on the arm. 'We are spoiled, aren't we?'

He twinkled at her. 'We are indeed.'

Gill escaped before they could ask any more awkward questions. She scurried along the hall and into the kitchen to put the cleaning things away. Luke was at the kitchen counter, chopping a cabbage into fine shreds with a wicked-looking knife. 'Are you pretending that's Harry's head?' she teased.

He smiled and carried on working. 'Quite possibly. Our work wore him out for a while and he's gone to shower again before lunch. I couldn't do anything other than ask him to join us. Sorry.' He stopped and gazed admiringly at her. 'How do you look so darn fresh all the time? No one would think you'd been cleaning rooms all morning.'

Gill blushed under his scrutiny. 'I bet you say that to all the girls.'

'I sure don't,' he said vehemently and quickly looked away, the back of his neck turning bright red.

Despite her intention not to encourage something that could never go anywhere, she experienced a frisson of pleasure. Shamefully, she admitted to herself it gave her ego a boost to have this handsome, intelligent man obviously flustered simply by being around her. The fact she behaved the same around him was much more disconcerting.

'What can I do to help?' she asked.

'Lay the table,' Luke replied, keeping his back to her. 'You can tell Betsy and Thaddeus we're about ready to eat. Harry should be down soon.'

'Will do.' She got busy gathering up cutlery and plates but couldn't stop from smiling as she made her way back out into the other room. This certainly wasn't proving to be the Christmas she'd expected. She'd imagined herself sulking and miserable in the middle of her sympathetic family while everyone avoided talking about her failed plans. Instead she hadn't had the time for anything resembling moping, and felt more alive than she had done in absolutely ages.

She ran down the hallway and knocked on Mr Walton's door before opening it. 'Lunch is ready. Would you like any help?'

Aunt Betsy smiled. 'I think we two

old crocks can help each other, thanks anyway.'

'We certainly can, my dear.' Thaddeus rose slowly to his feet and held out his arm for Betsy to hold on to as she stood to join him.

It suddenly struck Gill what a lovely couple they made, but almost as quickly she chided herself. They were both still grieving, and her aunt was a very sick woman. Gill had been cross at them when she thought they were trying to be matchmakers for herself and Luke, so she shouldn't do the same in return. She would keep her head down, work hard, get through the next couple of weeks, and head safely back home. Still, they were smiling so nicely at each other . . .

15

Gill finished her second barbeque sandwich and wiped a smear of spicy sauce from her mouth. 'That was delicious,' she declared, pushing away her plate before she could be tempted with any more.

'This is our standard Christmas Eve lunch,' Betsy said with a happy smile. Gill couldn't help thinking how much better her aunt looked after her sleep. Maybe coming back hadn't been such a bad idea after all. 'Hank was never a fan of turkey, so he said he needed something decent beforehand.' A shadow crossed Betsy's face and Thaddeus reached over to squeeze her hand.

'It's good to remember, my dear,' he said with a kind smile. 'It hurts, but it's better than forgetting.'

For a second Gill thought about Michael and the joy on his face when she'd accepted his proposal. She refused to accept his assertion that it'd been a huge mistake on both their parts. The fact they'd grown apart shouldn't be allowed to blot out all the good times they'd shared over the years.

'Are you all right?' Luke whispered by her side, and she turned to meet his gaze, his eyes so full of concern she had to swallow hard to avoid bursting into tears. 'Get today behind you and it'll get better.'

The blood drained from her face and she was afraid she might faint. All this time he must have known and had only been feeling sorry for her. No way would she let him see he'd got under her skin. She pulled back her shoulders and flashed him a bright, false smile.

'I'm absolutely fine, thank you,' she said in a loud, clear voice, and deliberately turned away to face Harry at her other side. 'Tell me all about the happy couple getting married tonight.' She intercepted anxious glances between her aunt, Thaddeus and Luke, but was determined not to back down. This should prove to them all she didn't need to be an object of their pity.

'Marti and Johnny are both old friends of mine and Portia's,' Harry explained. 'We grew up together in Silver Springs, Maryland. Our folks all worked inside the Beltway and were either in the military or politics. Johnny's a good guy, and he and Marti have been a couple forever.'

Gill bit back a sarcastic comment about that not necessarily working out in the long run. She mustn't judge others by her own standards. 'Will it be a large wedding?'

Harry grinned. 'Oh, yeah. Marti's father's up for re-election this year, so lots of people needed to be invited. Plus they're a social couple, so loads of friends on the list too.'

'I'm sure it'll be quite an event.'

He nodded. 'The party will go on all night, I'm sure.'

'Just be careful you don't end up snowed in,' Luke spoke up, and glared at Harry who had reached his hand across to rest on Gill's arm. 'Some of us have work to do.' He pushed back his chair and stood up, focusing on Gill. 'If you can manage to clear up lunch, I'll go and get busy in the kitchen.' He cracked a wry smile. 'Unless you'd rather bake a few pies and clean the turkey, that is?'

She wished she could take him up on the challenge, but wasn't totally stupid. 'I don't think so. I'm much safer with dirty dishes and leftovers.'

'Anything I can do to help?' Harry asked, and she realized he was still holding on to her hand.

'Thank you, but no. We don't make a habit of putting guests to work,' she said, hoping Luke overheard. 'You could watch TV until your girlfriend gets back.'

'Girlfriend?' He gave her a questioning look. 'You mean Portia?'

Who else do you think I mean? The Queen of England? 'Well, yes.'

He burst out laughing. 'Heck. Where

did you get that idea?'

From her. 'I suppose I assumed . . . ' Gill let her voice trail away, not wanting to spell out in front of everyone how Portia had laid claim to Harry the moment she arrived at the inn.

'We're good friends, nothing more, and have been forever. Sometimes she calls me her boyfriend because it's easier than explaining how we really are.' Harry flashed a quick grin. 'Now the delectable Helen could be another story, if I play my cards right tonight.' He oozed confidence, and Gill could see a cat fight on the horizon. From what she'd seen, Portia wouldn't give up anything to her half-sister, least of all a man she obviously regarded as hers.

Gill put her professional face back on. 'I must get on now.' She stood up and started to clear away. 'Would anyone care for coffee?'

'It's nap time for us old folks,' Betsy declared, and Thaddeus nodded his agreement. 'Tell Luke I'll be in later to make the chocolate pie. And if he argues, you can say I know he's capable of doing it, but I'm not ready to roll over and die just yet.'

'Oh, right.' Gill was at a loss how to reply. There wasn't much she could say without upsetting them both. She gathered up the tray she'd been loading and headed for the kitchen. Pushing open the swing door, she halted in her tracks at the sight of Luke standing over by the sink and obviously waiting for her.

'Come on in, I'm not going to bite,' he stated in a distinctly sharp tone of voice.

She stepped forward and let the door shut behind her. 'Before I forget, I've got a message from Aunt Betsy.' She repeated her aunt's words and watched Luke's jawline tighten. 'And before you start on me, I don't wish to discuss my ex-fiancé with you or anyone else.'

Luke's eyes narrowed. 'Fair enough. I never meant to offend you, and if you think I kissed you out of some sort of warped pity then you're a fool.'

Even from a distance she was acutely aware of his physical presence. If he dared to step any closer she might not be able to resist him.

'Could we please just get on with what needs to be done?' She heard the note of pleading in her voice and hoped he'd understand.

'Yeah.' His gaze travelled down over her, heating every inch of her skin. 'But we're not done, and if you think we are then you aren't the smart lady I believe you to be.'

There was no answer she could give that wouldn't be a lie, so she stayed silent and waited.

'I'll give in for now,' Luke announced with a shrug, but for some reason Gill didn't feel as though she'd won.

*   *   *

Three hours later Gill collapsed onto the nearest kitchen stool with a worn-out sigh. Spread out on the countertops around her was a huge amount of food ready for their Christmas meal. Pecan, apple, and pumpkin pies. Coconut cake. Cornbread dressing to go with the massive turkey Luke had cleaned and placed back in the fridge ready to cook tomorrow. There was a sweet-potato casserole, plus a green-bean casserole Luke assured her was a staple of every southern holiday meal. She'd been entrusted with making the cranberry sauce, something simple he convinced her she could do. Even she couldn't mess up heating sugar, water and cranberries until the fruit popped and was soft. Apart from that, she'd done basic tasks like chopping apples and washing lots of dishes.

'Are you ready for a cup of tea?' Luke laughed, and put the kettle on without waiting for her to reply. They'd eased back into their usual friendly banter, but she'd missed his easy touches on her arm and the way he used to stand a little closer than necessary while they worked.

Just as well, she told herself, without being convinced.

'If you're good, we'll taste-test some of the snickerdoodle cookies,' he said, pointing to the sugar cookies topped with a selection of cinnamon sugar or red and green sprinkles. They were made from one of Hank's old family recipes, and Betsy wouldn't consider it Christmas without them.

'Are you sure we can spare a couple?' Gill replied with more than a touch of irony.

'Maybe. After we've had our tea I'll let Betsy come in and make her chocolate pie.' He looked thoughtful as he poured the boiling water into the teapot. 'What do your family do for the holidays?'

Gill played along and told him all about their traditions. They usually met friends on Christmas Eve at the local pub for a couple of drinks before going to church for the midnight service. She ran through everything they ate for their Christmas dinner, telling him about the decorative crackers on the table with their paper hats and bad jokes. 'After we've cleared up, we listen to the Queen's speech at three o'clock and then open all our presents.'

'You have to wait until then? Sounds cruel to me,' he commented with a smile.

'When did you open yours as a child? Earlier, I suppose?' she asked, and it was as though a steel shutter crashed down over his face.

'There were rarely any presents in the homes I was in.' His terse explanation tore at her heart. She wished she had the nerve to wrap her arms around his neck and tell him she was sorry, but he'd no more accept pity than she'd wanted to earlier. He jumped back up. 'You go ahead and finish your tea, and I'll get Betsy in here.'

Gill let him go for now. She had a lot to mull over.

16

'You can't be serious!' Gill exclaimed.

Luke finished fastening the buttons on his heavy outdoor coat and then pulled a black knitted cap down over his head. 'Hank always grilled steaks on Christmas Eve.'

'But it's freezing cold out there and getting worse by the minute,' she said, exasperated by his insistence on cooking massive T-bone steaks on the outside grill for their dinner. The weather had deteriorated during the afternoon, exactly as the TV forecasters and Luke had predicted. Their guests had gone off to the wedding, all dressed to the nines, and Gill had watched them leave with more than a touch of relief. Thanks to Luke, she'd been able to produce the requested snacks before they left. The list of things she owed him was growing rapidly.

'You'll catch your death of cold,' she tried one last time.

'Give me a break. I'm nearly thirty-one years of age, for heaven's sake. Plus, the last time I looked, you weren't my mother.'

'I bet she'd say the same if she was here,' Gill retorted.

'We'll never know, seeing as I don't have a clue who she even was; and any woman who dumps a baby on the doorstep of a hospital probably isn't overflowing with maternal instincts.' Luke's heavy sarcasm hit her in the pit of her stomach and she slapped a hand across her mouth to stop from crying out. The silence between them was deafening, and neither moved.

'Don't say you're sorry, all right?' Luke snapped. 'You wouldn't let me show you any sympathy earlier, so you don't get to either.' He seized the tray of steaks and strode over to the door. 'Everything else is ready. All you have to do is fix the drinks. I'll be about a half hour.'

The door slammed shut behind him, and Gill slumped down on the nearest stool with Luke's revelation filling her head. Getting to know him was like putting together an extremely complicated jigsaw puzzle, and every time she thought she knew where a piece fitted she was proved wrong.

Mr Walton suddenly walked in, frowning when he saw her. 'Is something the matter, Gillian?'

'It's nothing to do with my broken engagement, if that's what you're thinking,' she said quickly, needing to put a stop to that notion before the conversation went any further. The older man coloured slightly and she wondered if she'd been too abrupt. 'Sorry, I didn't mean to be rude, but Aunt Betsy obviously told you about it.'

'It was mentioned, but only as one of the reasons why you were coming to help out,' Thaddeus explained kindly.

'I don't want to pretend it wasn't very upsetting at the time, but I honestly am okay with it now.' She wanted him to really understand, considering it practice for getting other people to believe her too. 'It's left me somewhat untrusting, more of my own judgement than of men in general.'

He rested a hand on her shoulder. 'That's only natural. Getting to know yourself is a long, painful process.' His eyes clouded over and Gill guessed he was remembering his wife. 'Worth it, though.'

'I hope so,' she said with a small laugh.

'So, why the long face when I came in?'

She held back for a second, unsure how much to say.

'Is it about our friend, Luke?'

She stared in amazement. 'How did you guess?'

Thaddeus chuckled. 'I may be somewhat closer to seventy than I care to admit, but I still have all my faculties. He's the only person who could have put that much sadness in your pretty eyes.'

The astute observation lit up her cheeks in a rush of embarrassed heat. She couldn't lie and deny her interest in Luke, so she took a deep breath and launched into the whole story. When she finished, she rested her hands on her lap and waited.

'I'd never heard about his mother, although I do know something of his background.' Thaddeus shook his head. 'I'd better stop there, my dear. Whatever he wants to reveal is up to him. He's a very private man, and for good reasons.' He gave her a sly smile. 'Of course, your aunt might not have as many scruples.'

'You surprise me,' she teased. 'Maybe we'll have the opportunity for a good chat when we're out in the cottage together.'

'Oh, I'm sure a smart young woman like yourself could make it happen.' His eyes shone with mischief, and Gill guessed this funny, interesting man must have attracted plenty of women in his day.

'I do believe I could,' she declared, and they both burst out laughing.

Luke popped his head in around the door and yelled 'five minutes' in Gill's direction before retreating back to the garden.

'Oops, we almost got caught out there,' she giggled. 'I've got twice-baked potatoes and salad to get on the table, plus our drinks. I'd better hurry up before he tells me off again.'

Thaddeus headed towards the door. 'I'll round up your aunt and we'll join you in a few minutes.' He pushed it open and glanced back at her. 'By the way, you might not be much of a cook, but the table looks mighty pretty tonight.'

Accepting compliments wasn't in her nature and Gill struggled to smile. She'd found a pretty red and green tablecloth in the linen cupboard and decided to use it for their meal. There was also a stack of red napkins, which she'd folded into fan shapes and arranged in the wine goblets.

'You have a real talent for flower arranging,' he insisted.

'It's just a few twigs and greenery from the garden,' Gill explained. She'd scoured the winter garden and cut a good selection, including shiny green holly laden with lush red berries. Rather than any sort of formal arrangement, she'd woven it all together to make a long runner down the centre of the table.

'So it might be, but it's beautiful, and once the candles are lit it will be quite a picture.' He glanced at his watch. 'Heck, we'll both be in trouble soon. I'll be back with Betsy.' He hurried off with a quick wave.

For a brief second, Gill wondered who would take over her job of laying the table at home for tomorrow's Christmas dinner. She might be banned from interfering with the cooking, but equally she never allowed anyone else to poke their nose into her table plans. Every year she went for a different colour and design. With the inn being so traditional, any of her more modern ideas would have been unsuitable. Tonight she'd chosen plain red candles, but she'd found a packet of gold ones in another drawer and would use those tomorrow.

As she set down the last salad bowl on the table, Betsy and Thaddeus walked in, chatting away happily. 'Well, bless my soul.' Betsy stopped and stared at the table. 'I heard it was a pretty sight, but hadn't expected all this. You're a sly one, I must say.'

Gill flushed under the rush of extravagant praise.

'Isn't she just?' Luke's deep, smooth voice behind her shoulder made her jump. The scent of his familiar cologne mixed with a hint of smoke from the barbeque sneaked into her awareness. He pulled off his hat, and Gill almost reached up a hand to smooth down his mussed-up hair but managed to stop herself just in time. He set down a large platter of sizzling steaks and then yanked off his coat, hanging it on the back of his chair.

'They look wonderful,' Betsy declared. 'Almost as good as Hank's.' Her voice cracked and Thaddeus gave her shoulder a quick squeeze.

'I learned from the master,' Luke murmured, glancing down at his feet.

For a moment a thread of sadness ran through the room, but then Betsy's smile returned. 'You did indeed, boy. Let's sit down and tuck in.'

Gill couldn't imagine her aunt managing to eat even half of one of the enormous steaks. It was hard to miss the fact that she picked at her food, pushing it around the plate a lot without actually eating much at all. Betsy had declared it the fault of the medicines taking away her appetite.

In a few minutes everyone had their plates dished up, and Thaddeus raised his wine glass. 'To absent loves. May they always be in our hearts.' He spoke softly, and they all joined in the toast.

Gill took a sip of the mellow red wine and glanced across the table, only to catch Luke's bright green eyes fixed on her. She lost the ability to breathe and held his gaze, allowing herself the pleasure of drowning in the emotions he wasn't attempting to hide.

'You cook a mean steak.' Thaddeus's contented voice broke through the moment and Gill forced her attention back to the meal.

'Thanks.' Luke's terse reply betrayed his own similar struggle.

She smiled to herself and picked up her knife and fork, oddly happy with the way the day was going.

17

Gill noticed Luke glancing anxiously out of the window. 'Is it getting worse?' The snow had been falling ever since they ate. They'd finished clearing up and moved over to sit on the sofas over by the Christmas tree to drink their coffee and make the most of the blazing log fire.

'Yep. I'm not too bothered, because I'm sure the Mockingbird can find three sleeping bags on the floor for our diva guests,' he joked. 'We've got enough food here; we're not going to starve.'

'That's hardly likely with the amount you cooked this afternoon,' she teased back at him.

Luke focused his attention on Betsy. 'I'd be happier if you came in here to sleep tonight.' He nodded back at Gill. 'And you too, of course.'

'What about you?' Gill asked. One day he'd pointed out to her his own small house on the slope behind the inn when they were standing at the back door. He'd never issued an invitation to see it and she'd refused to ask.

'I'll camp out in here too. Better we're all together. If we get ice forming on the power lines, next thing we'll have no electricity,' Luke explained.

'Oh, I hadn't thought of that.'

'Don't worry.' He smiled and draped his arm lightly around her shoulder.

They'd ended up together on the same sofa after Betsy and Thaddeus laid claim to the other one first. Gill couldn't help thinking they'd been out-manoeuvred again. If she were sensible, she would shift away, but the warmth of him pressed against her was too comforting to give up.

'I won't. I'm sure you'll keep us all safe,' she said lightly and his fingers tightened, digging into her soft flesh and startling her.

'Always. I wouldn't let any of you

down.' Luke's fierce reply sounded almost ridiculous; but seeing the dead serious expression on his face, Gill didn't dare to laugh.

'We know that,' Betsy piped up. 'You never have done.'

Gill knew there had to be unsaid volumes behind *that* comment. Luke caught her eye and looked a little shamefaced.

'Enough of all that. Betsy, what game is it going to be tonight?' Luke asked. 'We always play either cards or a board game,' he said to Gill, 'and it's always your aunt's choice.' It went unsaid that it had been Hank's rule.

Betsy briefly looked thoughtful, but then a mischievous smile tugged at her lips. 'I think it has to be Scrabble.'

'Oh, heck, anything but that,' Luke groaned.

'What's wrong?' Gill asked. 'It's a fun game.'

'Not the way your aunt plays. She's a fiend. Trust me, she'll destroy us all,' he said in a loud whisper, smiling over at Betsy.

Gill decided this wouldn't be the right time to mention she'd been her family's undisputed Scrabble champion for years. 'I'll be at a disadvantage because you spell so many things differently.'

'To make it fair, I say we accept either American or British spellings tonight,' he suggested.

Betsy shrugged. 'Doesn't bother me. By the way, Gill, has your mother got any better at playing? She was always hopeless.' The implication was that her daughter would be equally bad.

She shook her head, not adding that her mother refused to play with her anymore.

'Put some Christmas music on, Luke, dear, and then let's get started,' Betsy said, giving him a broad smile. 'We would usually go to church, Gill, but I'm not up to it this year.'

'Don't worry. Staying here in the warm will be fine with me.' She didn't say how glad she was not to have to go to a service tonight. Despite her reconciliation with the idea of her cancelled wedding, it might be wiser not to push herself too far. Her abiding love for the Christmas season had led her to insist on marrying then because the combination of beautiful decorations and her favourite carols was perfect in her eyes.

Luke got up to organize everything and soon the strains of 'Frosty the Snowman' resonated through the room, making everyone smile.

An hour later, Betsy wasn't smiling anymore. 'You are one very devious girl,' she declared, fixing Gill with a stern stare. ''Mazurka' on a triple word score. 'Sylph' using no vowels. And what did you say 'qadis' meant again?'

'It's an Arabic word for a judge appointed by the sultan,' Gill replied, suppressing the smile threatening to break through.

Luke's loud guffaw broke the ice and the next second Thaddeus joined him, laughing so hard Gill was afraid he'd burst something. Betsy glared at both men and that finished Gill off. She succumbed to a fit of giggles.

'Fancy taking advantage of a sick woman.' Betsy tried to sound plaintive, but no one took any notice. 'Luke Sawyer, go and pour me a large glass of Jack Daniels.'

'You're taking a lot of pills. Is it all right to — '

She stopped him mid-sentence with a wave of her hand. 'Don't argue. It's Christmas.'

He shrugged. 'Okay, you're the boss. Would anyone else like something? There's wine, beer or sodas.'

'Coke for me please, Luke,' Thaddeus replied with an apologetic smile at Betsy.

'A glass of wine would be lovely. White if you have it.' Gill jumped up from the sofa. 'I'll give you a hand.' She caught Betsy and Thaddeus looking and was almost tempted to stick her tongue out at them. Before they could make any smart remarks, she followed Luke out to the kitchen.

'You deserve a whole bottle after that little performance,' Luke joked as she walked through the door. '*I'll be at a disadvantage because you spell so many things differently.*' He mimicked her so accurately it was uncanny. 'If that was you at a disadvantage, I'd hate to see you at full throttle,' he observed with a decided smirk.

'Would you really?' Gill said, purposely fluttering her eyelashes in a half-joking attempt to flirt.

Luke set down the two cans of soda he'd got from the fridge and stepped towards her. The intensity in his eyes made her heart race. He stopped close enough for her to feel the heat from his body, but far enough away that they weren't quite touching.

'I don't know how to play this game, Gill.' The rasp in his voice sent shivers rippling down through her. She took a chance and reached up to stroke her fingers down the side of his face, rubbing against the soft, dark stubble shading his skin.

'Is that what we're doing?' she whispered.

'You tell me. You started it.' He almost sounded angry, but she knew it wasn't at her so much as the confusion she shared with him.

'Did I? I seem to remember you kissing me first.'

'Does it matter?' he pleaded, planting his hands on her shoulders so there was no chance of her moving away.

So many questions hung in the air between them, but right now all Gill cared about was making the most of this moment. There would be time for the rest later.

'You're so very lovely,' he murmured, pressing a gentle trail of kisses starting at her forehead all the way down to her neck. 'I've never seen the attraction of glossy, high-maintenance women.' He kissed his way back up to her mouth.

Gill arched into his touch and sighed. 'You know, some women would find that comment insulting.'

He pulled back and gave her a

puzzled frown. 'Why?'

'Because it implies I'm plain and ordinary,' she teased. 'Of course, I am, but — '

Luke silenced her with a fierce, hard kiss, wrapping his arms around her waist and pulling her closer. Gill could only give herself up to him until he finally let go.

'Plain and ordinary?' he scoffed. 'You want compliments, I can give you plenty. How about smooth, perfect skin, eyes sparkling with intelligence and good humour, soft brown hair I want to run my hands through — and then there's your delectable figure that I'd like to — '

'Shush!' Gill protested, her face flaming with embarrassment. She turned around, anxiously looking at the door. 'Behave yourself and let's get the drinks before the cavalry come to see what we're getting up to in here.'

A slow, lazy grin spread across his handsome face. 'Sure thing, sweetheart. Whatever you say. All I'm saying is that plain and ordinary you ain't, and it scares me half to death.' His drawl deepened and he gave a mischievous wink before letting go of her.

No man had ever flustered her this way before. Her relationship with Michael was always steady and calm; after all, they'd started as best friends, and it'd grown from there over many years. A picture flashed through her mind of Michael staring at his new girlfriend with the same intensity she'd seen in Luke's eyes, and it shook her to the core. This was a rebound thing, nothing more. It had to be. Didn't it?

18

'You kids can stay up as long as you like, but I'm beat,' Betsy declared with a gaping yawn.

'I'll hang around here until our guests roll back in,' Luke said. 'I can stretch out on the sofa if I get tired.'

'I'm sure Gillian will be happy to keep you company.' Thaddeus's eyes twinkled with mischief. 'She doesn't look the least bit worn out.'

Throw me at him, why don't you? Things were happening too fast, and the fear of doing something stupid on the rebound increased with every one of Luke's kisses. Gill had never been reckless where men were concerned, but being around him lowered her resistance.

'Looks can be deceptive. I'm guessing she'd rather head on to bed as well.' Luke's easy reply was belied by the way he fixed his attention on her. He was giving her the chance to turn down the suggestion with no hard feelings.

'I am pretty beat, actually. Let's get settled in our new room.' Gill looked straight at her aunt — anything to avoid Luke's scrutiny.

She had moved in everything they needed for tonight from the cottage earlier in the evening, purposely sneaking in the photo album ready for some gentle interrogation when the moment was right. Before there could be any more discussion, she stood up and prepared to help her aunt. Of course Thaddeus beat her to it, and had his arm at the ready before she crossed the room.

'You run on, dear, and we'll be with you shortly,' he dismissed her kindly.

'All right.' She glanced back over at Luke. 'Good night.'

He didn't answer, only gave a curt nod and returned to staring at the fire. Gill didn't know what she wanted, but it wasn't to leave him this way. There was no choice now, though, so she quickly left before she could do something even more stupid.

Gill made it to their room, the Magnolia Suite next to Mr Walton, and unlocked the door. She needed to open out the sofa to turn it into her bed for the night so Aunt Betsy could have the double bed to herself. Without letting herself think too much, she shifted the coffee table out of the way, then pulled the cushions off the sofa so she could stretch out the frame and unroll the thin mattress. Once the clean sheets were on, she hurried into the bathroom for a quick wash. Through the closed door she heard her aunt and Thaddeus talking and saying good night. A wave of tiredness swept through Gill, consoling her that she hadn't completely lied to Luke. Changing into her warm pyjamas, she started to remove her makeup and unconsciously smiled at her reflection in the mirror. *Definitely plain and ordinary now.*

'Gill, dear, can you come here and

give me a hand with my shoes?'

She sighed. 'I'll be right out.' Betsy might try to question her, but she'd had enough talking for one day and was ready to crawl into bed.

*   *   *

Gill jerked upright, completely disoriented and wondering where on earth she was. Through the tired fog in her brain, a strange noise hummed into her consciousness and made her heart thump.

Ella's moans have woken many a guest from a good night's sleep. Luke's words echoed through her head and a scream lodged in her throat as the door inched open.

'Gill, are you awake?'

'Who's there?' she whispered, her voice quavering with fear.

'It's Luke. Who did you think it was — Ella McBride?' Ribald laughter ran through his voice and she could have cheerfully hit him for frightening her half to death.

She scrambled from the bed and crept over to the door. 'Of course not,' she hissed. 'Do I look that gullible?'

'Nope, but you sure do look cute when you've just woken up, all crumpled and warm,' he teased, and glanced down at her bare feet. 'No bunny slippers tonight?'

'I didn't have time to put them on,' she snapped. 'I assume you didn't come here to check on my night attire.'

'I give in.' He held up his hands in surrender. 'Put me in detention and keep me in after school.'

'For goodness sake, stop being an idiot. What do you want, apart from interrupting my sleep?'

Luke's expression instantly turned serious. 'I just got a call from your other admirer, Harry. They were on their way back here in the Mockingbird's minivan earlier than they planned because of the snow, but it skidded off the road. A tow truck is trying to get to them, but with all the other wrecks going on he's not sure how long it will be. The snow's still coming down pretty hard, so I've offered to go pick them up. Doesn't do the inn's reputation any good if we have guests freeze to death.'

'Surely you won't be safe either?' She frowned, wanting to tell him not to be an idiot.

'My truck will be fine; it's not a problem,' he sought to reassure her. 'All I need you to do is get some hot soup and coffee ready for when I get them back here. Can you manage?'

'Of course. I'll leave a note for Aunt Betsy in case she wakes and wonders where I am.'

'Good idea. I'm guessing it'll take me a good half hour to get there and back, and that's with no holdups. Don't worry if I'm longer. I doubt my cell phone will work, so I probably won't be able to call you,' he explained patiently.

'Okay. I'll throw some clothes on then be out there.' She ached to tell him to be careful but didn't want him calling her a nag.

He touched the side of her face,

resting his warm hand against her cheek. 'And yeah, I'll be careful.'

'Good,' she whispered, no longer surprised at him guessing her thoughts.

He turned and left, and she closed the door behind him before padding across the floor to the chair where she'd abandoned her clothes before bed.

'What was Romeo after?' Betsy asked from the bed.

'Goodness, you startled me.' Gill jerked around to face her aunt. 'I didn't know you were awake.'

'I sleep lightly these days.' She sat up, turning on the lamp by her side. 'You didn't answer me.'

Gill decided to ignore the Romeo quip and gave a succinct version of Luke's story. 'So now you know as much as I do. I need to get dressed and get busy. Why don't you go back to sleep?'

Betsy pulled back the covers and swung her legs out over the side of the bed. 'Because it won't happen, Gillian. Once I'm awake that's usually it for hours. I'll come and give you a hand.'

'But you're supposed to be resting,' she tried to protest, but Betsy ignored her and carried on getting dressed. 'Fine, I give up.' She tossed her hands in the air and grabbed her own clothes and quickly started to pull them on.

'Good. Wise girl.' Betsy muted her sharp reply with a cheeky smile that Gill couldn't help responding to.

A tapping noise on the door made them both stop and look. 'Is something wrong, ladies?' Thaddeus asked from outside, and Gill flung open the door.

'What are you doing awake as well?' Gill felt like giving up. The idea of doing anything without everyone knowing around here was obviously impossible. If Luke *had* been trying to romance her, it would have been hopeless.

'The pain in my wrist woke me up and I couldn't get comfortable again, so I decided to read. I heard voices and people moving around, so thought I'd better check on you both,' he said firmly, making Gill feel an absolute heel.

'I'm sorry we disturbed you.' She sighed and launched into the whole story again. 'If you want to join us, feel free.'

'Let's go,' Thaddeus declared, holding out his arm to Betsy, who took it with a smile.

Gill walked on ahead, turning lights on as she went, and left them to come at their own speed. In the kitchen she filled the coffee pot and turned it on before starting to look for soup to heat up.

'Top cupboard, you'll find several cans of vegetable soup,' Betsy pointed out as she came into the room. 'There's homemade soup in the freezer, but it'll take too long to defrost. If you turn the oven on we can warm up some rolls as well.'

'Sit here, my dear.' Thaddeus pulled out a chair and Gill was amazed when her aunt obeyed without arguing. 'Now you can tell young Gillian what to do without wearing yourself out.'

'How about throwing a few more logs

on the fire? It won't be totally out yet, so shouldn't take much to get it going again,' Betsy suggested.

'Good idea. I'll do that,' Thaddeus said with a nod.

'But your wrist?' Gill protested.

'There's nothing wrong with the other one.' He dismissed her response with a laugh and limped out of the kitchen before she could continue the conversation.

'Men won't be told, you know,' Betsy said with a slow shake of her head.

Nor will you. Gill officially gave up on both of them.

Ten minutes later, with the soup simmering and rolls staying warm in the bottom oven, Gill found trays for everyone, deciding it would be warmer to eat around the fire than at the dining tables.

'I wonder what the weather's doing now?' Betsy asked, and Gill shrugged. She'd been trying not to think about it because then she got to worrying about Luke even more.

'I'll check.' Reluctantly she unlocked the back door and walked out on the step. Icy cold wind and snow swirled around her face and she instantly jumped back inside, slamming the door shut. 'It's terrible. Much worse. I couldn't even see the path.' Tears pricked at her eyes and she blinked hard, trying not to show how frightened she was.

'Luke's a sensible boy. They'll be fine.' Betsy's reassuring words were dimmed by the quaver running through her voice.

'Yes, of course they will,' Gill pretended to agree, while the pit in her stomach deepened.

19

Gill clasped her hands tightly on her lap to stop herself from snatching the ticking clock off the mantelpiece and throwing it across the room. She glanced over at Betsy, slumped in Thaddeus's arms, and both of them fast asleep. She'd taken the soup off the heat an hour ago and removed the rolls from the oven. Getting up from the sofa, she wandered over yet again to look out of the window, shivering as a twist of wind blew in through the frame.

A thick layer of snow settled on the porch floor, too deep for Luke's salt to be having an effect anymore. In the glow from the twinkling Christmas lights she noticed ominous shards of ice forming on the power line stretching across to the river.

Oh, Luke, where are you? Gill didn't

want to cry — it wouldn't do anybody any good — but a single tear seeped out and trickled down her face anyway. Over the continual sound of the wind gusting in around the inn, she heard a different, deep humming sound and craned her neck to try to see further down the driveway. She eased open the door enough to stick her head outside and caught a glimpse of eerie yellowish lights through the swirling snow. The lights edged closer and then suddenly disappeared. Was she imagining things now?

A different, sharper noise startled her and she stepped onto the porch, shaking with the cold and fear of what was out there. 'Luke? Is that you?'

'Gill? We're here.' Luke's deep, strong voice rang out and she could have cried with relief. It must've been the truck's engine she'd heard along with seeing its headlights. Now she could make out other voices and heard footsteps thudding up the steps. Portia's pinched, white face appeared in front of her.

'Come here. It's all right, you're safe.' She held out her arms and the other woman stumbled into them. 'Let's get you inside.' Gill pushed open the door behind her and virtually shoved Portia in over the step. Helen appeared next, helped along by Harry. 'Are you two all right?'

'We've been better,' Harry replied with a rough laugh. 'You'd better have a bottle of whisky in there.'

'Sure do,' Luke answered from behind them and stepped onto the porch. Gill drank in the reassuring sight of him, calm and controlled as ever and apparently unscathed. 'Get inside before you freeze,' he remonstrated, shooing her back into the inn.

'There are warm blankets over by the fire. I'll go and heat the soup back up and resurrect the rolls. Luke can see to the whisky, that's his specialty.' She threw him a grateful smile and he grinned right back, making her heart race in the best possible way. With all the upheaval, Betsy and Thaddeus were awake, and everyone was now talking at once. Gill hurried off to the kitchen and went straight to the oven. Bending down to put more rolls in to warm, she screamed as two strong hands clamped around her waist.

'Hey, it's only me,' Luke joked.

She straightened up and turned to face him. 'I didn't know, did I? It could've been Harry the human octopus for all I know.'

Luke shook his head. 'I can see I need to improve my technique if you can't tell the difference.'

'This is *not* the place to waste time flirting, Luke Sawyer,' Gill insisted with a stern glare, but he popped a kiss on her forehead and shut her up.

'I'll go back to doing my duty in a minute, but I need a proper kiss first,' he declared with vehemence. 'It was the single thing that kept me going when I thought I was going to die in a blizzard.' His plaintive whine might have worked if he hadn't rolled his eyes far too dramatically.

'Never go on the stage. You'd be hopeless. The word 'overacting' leaps to mind,' she teased.

'Weren't you worried about me?' he said jokingly. His casually spoken words brought back the anguish of the last few hours and Gill's throat clamped around the emotions threatening to spill over. 'Oh, sweetheart, I'm sorry. Apart from Betsy and Hank, I'm not used to anyone thinking much about me.' He sighed and pulled her into his arms.

Nothing ever felt so solid and good, and Gill rested her head on his chest out of sheer relief. 'We need to get back out there,' she whispered, wishing they could be alone for once.

'Yeah, I know. Sort of doomed, aren't we?' he groused good-humouredly. 'Let's go and be good hosts. We'll make up for it later, I promise.'

She didn't dare to ask exactly what he meant, but a small streak of happiness unfurled in her gut. It was a feeling she hadn't experienced for a very long time.

★　★　★

Wearily Gill got ready for bed, again. Aunt Betsy was already asleep and snoring away happily. The glowing numbers on her alarm said it was now three o'clock. Portia and Helen weren't women to let an opportunity for drama to go by, and they'd relished having a captive audience. By the way Luke raised his eyebrows a few times, Gill guessed the story was getting more exaggerated by the minute. Harry had merely agreed with both of them while sinking a significant amount of whisky.

Thankfully, everyone agreed eight was far too early for breakfast, and it had been decided Gill would get some food ready by ten, but the kind that wouldn't hurt if it sat around for a while. Luke had suggested bagels and fresh fruit, seeing they'd be having a big meal later in the day, and offered to cook eggs on demand for anyone who wanted them. It was lucky he'd bought a huge turkey, because it was unlikely their guests would make it back to Mockingbird Farm unless the weather did a huge turnaround. Gill ordered herself not to fret over when they'd actually be able to leave. Her mother's prediction of a couple of days taking care of three guests and then a fortnight's house-sitting couldn't have been further from the truth.

She sighed and crawled into bed, shifting around so the metal frame didn't poke into her back. Then she pulled up the blankets, and Luke's handsome face was the last thing she saw before sleep pulled her away.

* * *

A loud ringing noise dragged her awake and she hurried to turn off the alarm before it woke her aunt as well. How could it be nine o'clock already? She dragged herself from the bed and into the shower. Blearily, she peered into the mirror and winced. Worry and not enough sleep had taken their toll, judging by the grey colour of her skin and the dark shadows rimming her eyes. It would take a decent makeup job to not frighten everyone she met today. She worked hard on her appearance for the next fifteen minutes and emerged, if not exactly bright-eyed and bushy-tailed, then at least less horrific.

She wandered down the hall and stopped to turn the Christmas tree lights on before going into the kitchen. She worked methodically and soon had everything sorted and under control. Fixing herself a large mug of tea, she went back out to get the fire lit and stopped in her tracks.

Over by the front door Luke stared out of the window, his profile seemingly etched in stone. She should probably leave him alone with his thoughts, but something in his silence drew her. Quietly she set her tea down on the table and walked across to join him.

'Happy thirty-first birthday to me,' Luke growled, almost to himself.

'I didn't know it was your birthday,'

Gill ventured. Of course there was no reason why she should, since he'd never opened up about himself apart from the one brief reference to his mother.

He shrugged. 'Probably is.'

'You're not sure?'

'A nurse at the Dallas Public Hospital found me outside around noontime and guessed I was only a few hours old, so it was an educated guess,' he murmured.

'She made sure you were somewhere safe; she didn't have to do that,' Gill ventured, still intimidated by his coldness.

'Very big of her.'

'Were there any clues who she might have been?' She might as well plough on; after all, he'd started this.

He pulled his worn leather wallet out of his jeans pocket and opened it out. 'Only this.' He fished out an exquisite heart-shaped pendant hanging from a fine silver chain and held it out to her. Wordlessly she took the necklace from his shaking hand and ran her finger over the initial 'S' etched in elaborate script, then opened the locket. Glancing up, she met his gaze.

'She was so young, and very beautiful.' The tiny picture was worn and faded, but Luke's resemblance to this girl with sparkling green eyes and jet-black hair couldn't be hidden. Gill passed the necklace carefully back to him. 'She must have loved you very much.'

'Strange way of showing it,' he snapped, jerking back around to stare out the window again.

'My guess, for what it's worth, is that her family didn't know, and for whatever reason she couldn't tell them. She plainly wasn't old enough to take care of you alone, and wanted you to have a better life,' she tried to reason with him while feeling his hopelessness. 'I assume the hospital tried to track her down?'

'Yeah. I checked a few years ago and found out they'd put pictures of the necklace all over the local media at the time with no response. Nobody was beating the doors down to admit any knowledge of me.' His voice was blank and expressionless.

There was so much Gill wanted to ask, but she sensed she needed to tread carefully. To someone with a close, loving family it was hard to fathom not knowing where you were from or having the built-in support system she couldn't imagine surviving without.

'She must have thought it was for the best. Did you end up with a good family?'

His rough, sarcastic laughter resonated through the room. 'We'll save that story for another day — like maybe never.'

Gill had never felt so far apart from Luke and couldn't see how to cross the chasm between them. 'Is this your way of saying you're giving up on us?' she asked. 'Because I'm getting that impression.'

'Anything between us was never going to work, Gillian,' he declared with a sad finality that made her want to scream. He took a step closer and reached up to cradle her face with his warm, muscular hands. She leaned into his touch, aching for him to say he was being an idiot and for her not to take any notice of him. Instead he pressed a soft kiss on her forehead and dropped his arms back down to his sides. Then he slowly walked away, dragging his boots on the polished wood floor.

'You're making a big mistake,' she shouted after him, and watched his broad shoulders tense up under his shirt; but he never turned around.

20

'Surely *I'm* not the first one down for breakfast?' Portia's loud voice on the stairs cut through Gill's musing.

'You are indeed. Happy Christmas!' She forced herself to at least sound cheerful.

'Wonderful, I'm sure,' Portia scoffed. 'Stuck here for goodness knows how long with my annoying half-sister and a boyfriend who doesn't appear to know where his loyalties lie.' She had dismissed Gill's effort to put a brave face on things with a few sharp words.

'I'm sure the roads will be clear soon.' Gill said, more for her own benefit, because the idea of being caged up in the inn much longer wasn't appealing to her either.

Thaddeus came to join them, smartly dressed for the day in grey slacks, a crisp white shirt, and a colourful

Christmas tie decorated with snowmen and holly. 'Very doubtful, ladies. The forecast is predicting another cold front coming through tonight that could bring ice as well as snow.' He shook his head. 'We might be lucky and it could go further north. There's no way of telling yet.'

'That's it. We must get out of here today,' Portia declared in her typical no-nonsense fashion.

Luke swung in from the kitchen, carrying a loaded tray. 'Only way you'll be doin' that is on skis, honey. The snow's not melting anytime soon, and we'll be lucky to get any ploughs out this far before tomorrow.' He set the food down on the table and started to unload the breakfast he'd put together.

Gill could have kicked herself. She'd been too caught up in their earlier conversation to remember why she'd got out of bed early in the first place. He must think she was completely incompetent. 'I'll go and get the coffee,' she said quietly.

'Sure.'

One word. Was that how it was going to be between them now? Gill caught Thaddeus looking curiously at them both, but she brushed past him without speaking, grabbed the coffee pot and headed back out.

'Merry Christmas, everyone.' Helen's cheerful laughter made them all look, which Gill guessed was exactly what the young woman wanted. Today she was startlingly lovely in a simple pale grey dress, given the perfect festive touch by a scarlet cashmere shawl draped artistically around her shoulders. Her red leather ankle boots added a touch of fun and whimsy.

Gill sneaked a glance over at Portia, startled by the coldness in her hard blue eyes as they landed on her half-sister.

Just then Helen turned and held out her hand to Harry, who appeared pale and haggard as he trailed down the stairs behind her. 'Come on, slow-coach,' she admonished him.

'Help yourselves to breakfast,' Gill announced brightly. 'Luke, what time will we be having our Christmas dinner?'

'The turkey's in cooking already, so around two, if that suits everyone?'

Nobody objected, and Gill didn't dare to ask when he'd got that done. She had the idea turkeys took a long time to cook, and the thing she'd watched him manhandling yesterday was massive.

'I'll fix a plate and take it to Betsy,' Thaddeus announced. 'I popped in to check on her and she was awake but still in bed.' A hint of colour warmed his cheeks. 'She's not up to joining us all yet.'

Gill was mad at herself again for not considering her aunt. Biting her lip, she caught Luke staring at her. He shook his head, telling her off again for being too hard on herself. That was a joke coming from him, because no one was harder on themselves than Luke.

'Of course.' She didn't offer to take

Thaddeus's place, pretty sure he'd rather see to Betsy himself.

The atmosphere hanging between her remaining three guests could be cut with a knife. Portia had chosen the chair at the end of the table and kept flashing venomous looks in Helen and Harry's direction. Helen prattled on about nothing in particular, seemingly oblivious to Portia's distaste. At the same time Harry kept his bleary eyes focused on the table, while taking occasional sips of black coffee and nibbling at a plain bagel.

'If there's anything else you need, just ring the bell,' Gill cheerfully announced, pointing to the antique silver bell in the middle of the table and hurrying off to the kitchen.

'There's nothing for you to do yet. You can help later,' Luke called out, keeping his back to her and methodically chopping vegetables.

'Oh, right.' *Make it a bit clearer you don't want me around.* 'I'll get some breakfast and go eat it out of your way.' She waited for him to say she could never be in his way, but he didn't respond. Stupid idea. She glanced at her watch. It was four o'clock in Cornwall now and a good time to phone. 'I'll take some time to ring my family too.' Immediately, she wanted to bite off her tongue. She couldn't have said a more tactless thing after their earlier conversation. Apologizing would only make things worse, so she carried on. 'Would you mind keeping an ear out for our guests?'

'No problem,' he grunted.

She felt like shaking him, but instead picked up a bagel and popped it in the toaster, then turned the kettle back on to make a fresh cup of tea. Five minutes later she left Luke to his sulk, determined not to let him totally spoil Christmas.

★   ★   ★

Gill closed up her phone and sighed. That had been harder than she'd expected. Hearing all her family laughing and joking without her tugged at her heart. She hoped she'd managed to reassure them that she was having a great time and staying busy. The busy part wasn't a lie, but the rest . . .

She'd avoided going into details about her aunt because Christmas Day wasn't the right time to tell her mother how sick her sister really was. Betsy was looking much better today, though. She'd taken some trouble with her hair, put on a little lipstick, and dressed in smart black trousers and a red sweat-shirt decorated with a glittery silver Christmas tree. Betsy and Thaddeus appeared to be helping to cheer each other up, and that had to be a good thing.

Her guests must be done with breakfast by now, so she'd better go and clear up the dishes before Luke did that as well. She made her way back to the big room and was surprised to see Harry sitting alone at the table.

'Do you mind if I clear up now?' she asked.

'Sure, go ahead. I'm done.' The bagel

on his plate was barely touched, but she didn't comment. 'Rum sort of Christmas, isn't it?'

'You could say that,' Gill replied with a sigh.

'By your cute accent I can tell you're not from around here, so how did you end up working at the inn?' he asked, taking another swig of coffee that had to be cold by now.

She laughed and gave him a brief explanation, telling him about her regular job and how she'd ended up here over the holidays. She skimmed over any reference to her broken engagement and instead emphasized her aunt's need for some help. 'What do you do?' She wanted to steer the conversation away from herself, because that was dangerous ground.

'According to Portia, very little,' he replied with a wry smile.

'Is she wrong?' Gill teased. It wasn't hard to imagine this handsome charmer living a playboy lifestyle. Harry's bright blue eyes darkened and narrowed as he focused on her, and a shiver of unease ran down her spine. 'Don't tell me you're really a nuclear physicist working on a top-secret project for the government?'

'Hardly.' He gave in to a short, harsh burst of laughter. 'Let's just say Portia's opinion of me was formed when I was a reckless young man and she's never seen beyond it.' He toyed with the salt shaker.

'I didn't mean to be nosy,' Gill apologized.

He reached out across the table and clasped her hand. 'You weren't. You just hit on a sore spot, that's all.' One of his captivating smiles came her way and Gill couldn't resist smiling back. 'I dabble in a few different things.'

I'll bet you do.

'Nothing reprehensible I can assure you.' Harry tried to sound offended. 'I help in my family's real estate business, sail competitively and . . . ' He studied her again and she held her breath, willing him to open up without knowing why, because she hadn't exactly done the same in return. 'I sometimes help out a friend of mine who's in the investigative business. He's an ex-marine and a bit rough around the edges, so if he's got a job that needs a little more . . . uh, finesse, shall we say, he calls me in.'

'It sounds fascinating. What's been your most interesting case?' Gill probed.

He frowned and thought for a moment. 'I guess it'd have to be tracking down a war criminal hiding out in suburban Virginia. He'd lived a perfectly respectable life since fleeing from Europe in nineteen forty-five, but was responsible for the deaths of at least two thousand people.' He gave her a quiet smile. 'That one was pretty darn satisfying, I'd have to say.'

'There's more to you than meets the eye, isn't there?' she ventured, and he burst out laughing.

'I should hope so. A pretty face doesn't leave much of a mark on the world, does it?'

'Try telling that to your lady friends,'

she joked, and then slapped her hand across her mouth. 'Oh goodness, I'm sorry. I don't know what came over me.'

Harry leaned closer and playfully tweaked her nose. 'I won't tell them if you don't. Personally, I value my life too much.'

'Me too,' she ventured with a half-smile, relieved his sense of humour stretched far enough to encompass her tactless remark. She checked her watch. 'I'd better get going. I've a lot to do.'

He immediately jumped up and pulled out her chair for her. Before she could thank him, she found herself pulled into his arms and being very thoroughly and competently kissed.

'You can come and help me — '

Gill glanced over Harry's shoulder and flinched as she met Luke's hard, unflinching stare. A movement on the stairs caught her attention, and she turned to see Portia and Helen staring at them with similar shock on their faces. *Happy Christmas.*

21

Gill wished Harry would stop grinning like a madman and let go of her, but he didn't seem in a hurry to end her embarrassment.

'I'll let you get on with your work.' He kissed her again, thankfully only on her forehead, and then shoved his hands in his pockets before strolling towards the stairs. 'I think it's time for a nap before lunch.' He edged his way around his fellow guests, whistling 'Hark, the Herald Angels Sing' as he took the stairs two at a time.

Gill tried to appear unfazed by the fact that three pairs of accusing eyes were now fixed on her. 'I'll bring the dishes in, Luke, and then I'm all yours.'

'Really? Could have fooled me.' He swung around and stalked off back into the kitchen.

She stood with her mouth gaping

open. Could the man be any more contrary?

'How many more men am I going to discover you kissing?' Portia said, obviously bemused.

This must be happening in some parallel universe. After having one boyfriend for a decade, Gill now appeared to be considered some sort of femme fatale. She compared her very ordinary appearance with the two glamorous women staring at her and had to stifle a giggle. Surely they couldn't be jealous of her? The idea was preposterous.

Helen linked her arm through Portia's. 'I think Harry's made fools of us both.'

'For once I believe you're right.' Portia's dislike of Gill was obviously stronger than that of her half-sister. She stared pointedly at her again. 'Would it be too much trouble for you to rustle up a bottle of white wine and maybe some olives and cheese? We'd like to have it over there.' She gestured towards the fireplace.

'Of course. I'll see to it right away.'

Gill gathered up the remains of Harry's breakfast and scurried away. Only as she pushed open the door did she remember Luke, and by then it was too late to retreat.

He was doing the maniacal chopping thing again. This time it was a bowl of carrots receiving the treatment. She was afraid to speak in case he was startled and lost a digit.

'You can open those cans of beans and drain them.' He pointed to several tins on the counter.

Gill sighed and explained Portia's request. 'I'd better do that first.'

'Yeah. After snatching her boyfriend, I suppose it's the least you can do,' he sniped. 'Of course, I'm not sure which sister he was dating, but I guess it doesn't matter now.'

Her blood ran cold. She'd had enough of his high-handed manner. Her family could have told him that she rarely lost her temper, but when she did it was best to watch out. She stepped closer to where he was working and placed her hands down on the counter-top in front of him.

'Now you listen to me.' His head jerked up and she fought against flinching. 'I've had enough of you and your unpredictable moods. One minute you're all over me like a rash, and the next you basically tell me to clear off.' Luke's jaw tightened but he didn't speak. 'Harry is a charming, friendly man who I find to be good company, nothing more. But frankly, it's none of your business.'

He glanced down at his vegetable pile. 'I'm sorry. My remarks were uncalled for.'

'Yes, they were,' Gill whispered, close to tears. 'Now I'm going to see to the wine, and then I'll be back to help you. I hope we can at least be polite to each other for the rest of my stay here?'

Luke laid down his knife and nodded. 'Yeah. I'm really sorry. I didn't mean for things to turn out . . . ' He choked on his words and went silent.

'I know,' Gill said sadly, and turned

away. With trembling hands she found a small silver tray and put together everything Portia had requested. She straightened her shoulders, headed for the door, and prepared for another showdown.

She was surprised to hear the two women laughing as she stepped into the other room. For a second she held back as they chatted happily together. She caught a mention of an ugly dress someone had been wearing at the wedding, and mutual admiration of how each other had looked. It was the first time she'd seen them as anything other than rivals. Maybe Harry's wandering eye had done them a favour after all.

'Here we go. Would you like me to pour you both a glass?' Gill wanted to dump the tray and run, but that wasn't on the cards.

'What we'd really like is for you to fetch another glass and join us.' Portia's frank comment took her by surprise and she didn't know how to reply without being rude.

'That's very kind of you, but I have to help get lunch prepared, and your rooms need cleaning,' Gill explained, relieved to be telling the absolute truth.

'But we insist,' Portia said, her face fixed in a glacial smile. 'Our rooms can wait, and I'm sure your handsome cohort in the kitchen will manage just fine for a few more minutes.'

'Uh, right. Thank you.' Gill quickly grabbed an ordinary juice glass from the old oak dresser over by the back wall and slowly made her way back to join her guests. This must be what Marie Antoinette felt like on the way to her execution. She opened the wine and filled three glasses, then passed the other women their drinks and perched on the edge of the sofa. Quickly she drained half of her wine in one long swallow to give her courage.

Portia spoke up first. 'We would like to know your intentions as far as Harry is concerned.'

Gill almost laughed, because it sounded exactly the way a Victorian father would ask questions of a man wooing his daughter. 'I'm afraid I don't quite understand.'

The two other women exchanged knowing glances. 'He's been my friend since childhood,' Portia continued, 'and I've often thought he might become more at some point. Harry and Helen have become friends too, but she and I have come to the conclusion that either of us dating him would be unwise.' She patted Helen's hand and managed a taut smile. 'Blood is thicker than water. Even if it is half-blood.'

Maybe Harry had done some good. Gill smiled inside at the idea of his flirtatious behaviour drawing this pair closer together. 'Please don't take this the wrong way, but I have no interest in Mr Warburton *that* way,' she answered.

'But he was kissing you!' Helen protested.

'Did you see me kiss him back?' Gill tossed out. 'No, you didn't. He's a charming, likeable flirt — end of story.'

A satisfied smile crept over Helen's

face. 'Good. That's what I thought. Porky wasn't convinced, but I told her Harry couldn't possibly be seriously interested in *you*.'

Gill didn't react to the obvious insult; she didn't have to defend herself to these two. Luke was another case entirely, but she would put him from her mind for now. She finished off her wine and stood up. 'Well, I'm glad we have that sorted. Now I really must get back to work.'

'Let him do the running.' Portia's blunt statement took her by surprise.

'Who?'

'The cute hunk in the kitchen. He may be handy at lots of things, but he's plainly a dead loss where understanding women is concerned. You must make him work to get you,' she continued, oblivious to Gill's embarrassment.

'We really don't, uh . . . It's not like that between us.' Explaining the weird, complicated relationship between her and Luke wasn't on the agenda.

Portia's sly smile made Gill's cheeks

heat up until she knew they had to be glowing brighter than a red traffic light. 'If that's the way you want to play it, fine, but we're not blind are we, Helen?' she declared, smoothing out an imaginary crease in her immaculate cream wool trousers.

'We definitely aren't, Porky.'

Gill couldn't believe it when Portia made no objection to the pet name. 'You can think what you like.'

Gill walked away, barely keeping her anger in check. Who did they think they were, analyzing her as if she were a bug under a microscope? She groaned to herself. Now she had to go and help Luke whether she liked it or not.

'Green beans.' He barely glanced around from stirring a large saucepan on top of the oven. He picked up a spoon and tasted his cooking, adding a few pinches of salt. 'Later I want to bring the oil lamps in from the shed and fill them just in case.'

Gill started to open tins and dumped the beans into a colander in the sink to drain. 'Are you expecting the power to go off?'

'Depends which way this storm decides to go. But more snow and ice on top of what we already have is bound to break some lines.'

'You don't sound worried.' She frowned and set aside the empty tins.

He shrugged. 'We're prepared. We'll be fine. It's an inconvenience, nothing more.'

'You're good at this sort of thing, aren't you?' Gill asked. A slight flush crept up the back of his neck and she sensed she'd embarrassed him.

'I learned early on that the only person I could rely on was myself. Teaches you the hard way,' he murmured and turned to her, his face hard and sad. 'Being here with your aunt and uncle helped, but it never goes away.'

Gill's heart broke.

22

'Here we are, two more volunteers to help with Christmas dinner,' Thaddeus announced from the doorway, and Gill turned to see him and Betsy coming into the kitchen. 'We thought you might have other things to do, Gillian, and that Luke could maybe do with a couple of extra pairs of hands.'

She tried to pull herself together enough to reply and didn't dare to look at Luke. 'That would be great. I ought to see to the bedrooms.' Anything to get out of here. She was sure Luke wouldn't want to continue the previous conversation, but she couldn't have stayed here and ignored it as though nothing had been said. 'I'll be finished in plenty of time to lay the table. Nobody else is to touch it,' she said with a smile. Before anyone could object, she wiped her hands and almost ran from the kitchen and on up the stairs.

In the safety of Portia's quiet room Gill worked away steadily, first making the bed and then starting on the bathroom. Scrubbing the toilet allowed her to think about other things. She couldn't get past Luke's story about his mother's abandonment. The desire to discover the truth must be in his head all the time, and she suspected until he found out who his mother was a large part of him would always be closed off.

I sometimes help out a friend of mine who's in the investigative business. Gill smiled, remembering Harry's explanation of one of his jobs. Why hadn't it occurred to her before? She'd ask him for help. Picking up her duster, she sprayed cleaner on the mirror and wiped away several smeary marks. She then started on the washbasin, but halted mid-scrub. Luke would never forgive her if she told his story to anyone else, especially Harry. It was an idiotic idea, and one she needed to forget.

But what if I can do it without him knowing? She cared for him — too much, if she were to be honest — but even if things weren't going to work for them as a couple, at least she could maybe do this for him. She made herself concentrate on her work, and with fresh towels hung up and the bins emptied she headed next door to Helen's room to repeat the whole process.

When she was done, Gill looked at her watch and hesitated. The downstairs bedrooms still hadn't been touched, so she'd get them out of the way and come back to do Harry's later when he wasn't in. Suddenly the nearest door opened and his smiling face popped around.

'I thought I heard someone out here, and see how lucky I am — it's you. Do you want to come in and do whatever cleaners do?' He opened the door back and waved her in.

For a second Gill wasn't sure, but quickly decided he wasn't likely to pounce on her again after the earlier disaster. Plus, it might help make her mind up about the Luke dilemma. 'Are you sure I won't be in your way?'

'Not at all. I could do with some company.' His bright blue eyes sparkled. 'I don't think anyone else is talking to me.'

'Um, well, okay,' she said with a nod, and walked past him carrying her cleaning supplies. 'Please carry on with whatever you were doing.'

He lounged against the door and gave her a lazy smile. 'I was about to change for lunch, but I believe I'll wait.'

She managed an awkward smile. 'Good idea.' She walked across the room and stripped the bedclothes back before smoothing out the bottom sheet and starting to remake the bed. She glanced up to see him sprawled on the red velvet armchair by the window, watching her intently.

'Did they all have a go at you after I left?' he asked.

Gill didn't answer straight away. With

the bed finished, she picked up her duster and freshened up the bedside tables and the top of the dresser. 'A little, but it was all right in the end.'

'With Luke too?' Harry probed.

'Sort of.' She stopped what she was doing to face him. 'I've got a hypothetical question to ask you.'

He propped his feet up on the coffee table with a decided smirk on his face. 'Not a proposal of marriage I hope?'

'Good grief, no!' she said in horror.

Harry burst out laughing. 'I didn't think so. Just making sure. Go on then.'

'If someone was abandoned as a baby and wanted to track down their birth mother, but they didn't have a name to go on, where would you start looking?'

He sat up and leaned forward to rest his elbows on his bent knees. 'Has this hypothetical person got any clues at all — say, a possible date or location?'

Gill nodded. 'They know the date they were, uh, left, and where it was. They also have a piece of jewellery that was left with them.'

'You mentioned your family in England earlier. I haven't done a lot of international work. I'm guessing you were adopted?' he asked.

'Certainly not. I'm not talking about myself,' she protested.

'People who ask the hypothetical question thing, or come to us saying they're asking on behalf of a friend — ninety-nine times out of a hundred they're talking about themselves,' Harry explained with unexpected kindness.

'If that's true, then I'm the one out of a hundred. I honestly am talking about someone else,' Gill insisted. His expression didn't change, so she guessed he wasn't convinced, but that didn't matter for now.

'Hypothetically, it might be possible to find out something. Is this piece of jewellery particularly distinctive?' he asked.

There was still time to retreat and stop all this. If she carried on much further, there would be no going back, and she might irretrievably damage her relationship with Luke. But could it really be much worse, anyway? She perched on the edge of the bed and took a few calming breaths to steady her racing heart. 'It's a good-quality silver pendant with an initial engraved on the front and a photo inside.'

'Can you get hold of it for me to see?' Harry questioned her, and she almost kissed him. For the first time he seemed to genuinely believe she was telling him the truth.

'It might be tricky, but I can give it a go.' She wasn't sure how to part Luke from his wallet, but she'd give it her best try. She ploughed on. 'The other piece of information I have is that it was at the Dallas Public Hospital on Christmas Day, nineteen eighty-two.'

'Are we talking about a boy or girl baby?' He appeared to take her fantastical story in his stride. Gill respected him for not once asking who she was talking about.

'A boy.'

He picked up a worn black leather notebook from the table and a gold fountain pen, then scribbled away for several minutes and smiled over at her. 'I'll do what I can. The necklace will really help.'

'What do you charge?' she blurted out. 'I'm sorry, I didn't think about that before, and I don't have a ton of savings, but I — '

He reached out to press a hand over her mouth. 'Shush. Consider this a Christmas present.' She tried to protest, but he only pressed harder. 'I'm not short of money, and I like you, okay?' He relaxed back in the chair again and stretched out with his hands behind his head. 'Plus I enjoy a puzzle, and I don't have much on at the moment. It'll keep my mind active.'

'Thanks,' Gill said awkwardly. 'I'll, um, clean your bathroom.'

'You do that, sweetheart, and I'll enjoy watching you,' he teased.

'You're impossible.'

'It's been said before,' he declared without any hint of shame.

Gill decided she'd better get working

or he'd never stop his ingrained habit of flirting with any living, breathing female within a five-mile radius. She hurried into his bathroom and gave it a very quick clean before coming back out.

'I'm off. See you later,' she announced, and quickly flung open his door only to walk straight into Luke's hard chest. 'Oh!'

'Betsy was looking for you — something about candles for the table. We didn't know where you'd got to.' He stared over her shoulder and the grim expression on his face darkened.

Gill turned to see Harry standing by the window with his shirt undone and a big smirking smile plastered all over his face. Her heart sank down to somewhere near her toes, the toes now curling up with embarrassment. She faced Luke and tried to smile. 'I just finished cleaning Mr Warburton's room.'

'I'm sure you did.' Luke's terse comment made her cringe. He stalked off towards the stairs without another word.

'Thanks very much,' Gill snapped at Harry. 'That was really helpful.'

'Anything to oblige, sweetheart.' He bent down to take off one of his socks and glanced up with another wicked smirk.

She stuck out her tongue at him, slammed the door shut behind her and hurried away. With her foot on the top step, she stopped and grabbed hold of the banister post, girding herself to face everyone again.

23

Gill set down her knife and fork with relief. She was amazed she'd got through the last couple of hours in one piece. Everyone else around the table was talking and laughing and didn't appear to have noticed her own distracted manner. Even Luke looked more relaxed, although he'd refused to discuss Harry with her earlier, saying they had too much to do. In a way she'd been relieved, but it hadn't solved anything.

'You did a wonderful job with the table, Gill dear,' Aunt Betsy declared. 'The candles fit in perfectly.'

Gill was pleased she'd brought a smile to her aunt's face. Betsy had produced the green and gold candles that afternoon and said Hank had bought them on sale after last Christmas. Yesterday's greenery was still fresh, so she'd entwined it with some gold gauze ribbon to make it look more cheerful. 'They're beautiful,' she agreed.

'It was a great meal,' Harry spoke up, and raised his wine glass. 'A toast to the cooks. You didn't expect to have us all here, and we appreciate the huge amount of trouble you've gone to.'

Luke managed a tight smile. 'It was no trouble.'

Helen chimed in with her own thanks, and Portia followed suit with only the faintest hint of reluctance.

'When do you think they'll get the roads clear enough for us to get out of here?' Portia ventured.

'It's hard to know for sure,' Luke said with a shrug. 'Could be by around lunchtime tomorrow; but if another storm comes in, I'm guessing at least a couple more days.'

'This is very inconvenient,' she griped. 'No offense to you all, of course,' she backtracked.

'Well, let's make the best of it, dear,' Betsy piped up. 'Why don't you all go and sit by the fire, and I'm sure my helpers will bring around coffee and dessert.'

'Good idea,' Luke declared, quickly standing up. He caught Gill's eye. 'Are you coming?'

'Of course.'

While everyone else shifted, she silently got up and began to take the dirty dishes into the kitchen. She didn't try to interfere as Luke set up the coffee tray and put several of the pies and cakes on pretty plates to take into the other room. After getting the dish-washer loaded, she washed her hands and turned to face him.

'What can I do now?' she asked.

'Take the plates, napkins and forks in and pass them around.' No please or thank you, simply a barely polite order.

She didn't bother to reply, just did what she was told. She put on a smile and helped to serve everyone, but when her aunt suggested she sit down and join them, she knew she couldn't fake it any longer.

'If you don't mind, I'm going to lie

down for a while. I've got a slight headache,' she said apologetically. 'I probably had too many glasses of wine.' She met Luke's quizzical expression but didn't flinch. No doubt the super-observant man was well aware she'd barely sipped at one glass and drunk water all the way through the meal.

'Of course, Gillian. I'll probably join you in a while. I'm fading too,' Betsy declared.

Gill wished they were back out in the cottage where she had her own bedroom, but couldn't say much. She supposed she shouldn't assume Luke was okay with hanging around, but couldn't bring herself to care too much about his sensibilities right now. While the going was good she made her escape and made it to her room unscathed, closing the door behind her with a huge sigh of relief.

She pulled off the smart black trousers and red blouse she'd been wearing all day and tugged on an old pair of grey sweatpants and a baggy green jumper. A smile tugged at her mouth as she shoved her feet into the infamous bright pink bunny slippers that had totally bemused Luke. Then she slumped down on the sofa and rested her head in her hands. Sleep wouldn't come to her even if she could be bothered to pull out the bed, not while her mind was such a swirl of conflicting emotions. Harry was simple — an incorrigible flirt. He wasn't to be taken seriously, and that was fine. Luke was another story, and one she couldn't decipher for the life of her.

Without thinking, she reached for the photo album and opened it again at the first picture of Luke with her aunt and uncle. She idly traced over his face with her finger. 'What happened to get you here?'

'Are you talking to yourself, Gillian, dear?' Betsy was standing in the doorway, holding a small tray. 'They say it's the first sign of old age.'

'I must be about ninety in that case,' Gill answered wryly, and her aunt laughed.

'You look pretty good for an old woman.'

'Plenty of makeup,' Gill joked.

'I've brought us some tea.' Betsy came in and closed the door. 'I figured you could maybe do with a cup. You even get to share my secret stash of Hobnobs.'

Gill jumped up to take the tray from her and set it down on the table. 'You're a lifesaver.'

They got themselves settled and the tea poured. There was so much Gill wanted to ask her aunt, but she didn't know where to start.

'Men are tricky creatures,' Betsy declared, nibbling at a biscuit.

'Was Uncle Hank?' Her aunt's eyes glazed over and for a second Gill was afraid she'd upset her.

'Yep. Most of them would usually prefer to have all their teeth out without anaesthetic than tell us how they feel about anything.'

Gill's tea went down the wrong way and she fought to keep breathing through a fit of coughs. Finally she was able to reply. 'Michael wasn't happy for ages but didn't know how to tell me. He let it go until we had the church booked and all the wedding arrangements made.'

'What prompted him in the end?'

'He met someone else.' She forced out the words, wondering when it would get any easier.

'Was he the only one who had blinkers on?' Betsy probed.

'Not really.' She shook her head. 'If I'm honest, I was no better. I closed my eyes to the fact we rarely had fun together anymore and never really talked about anything other than wedding plans.'

Betsy nodded. 'It usually takes two. Hank always said I talked too much,' she said with a laugh. 'I admit I could be a bit of a nag at times.'

'But it didn't pull you apart?'

'No. If it's the right person, then in the end it's all part of what makes up the fabric of your love. It's nothing to do with romantic dinners or flowery words. It comes down to holding someone's head while they're being sick or sticking with it even when they're being an idiot. If you're lucky, you'll find the one who will still be able to make you laugh after decades together.' She went suddenly quiet and Gill reached over to squeeze her hand.

'You must miss him terribly.'

'Yes,' Betsy murmured. 'But it doesn't mean I'm not thankful every day for the wonderful years we had. I wouldn't change a thing.'

Tears pushed at Gill's eyes, but she wasn't sure who they were for.

'He's a good man,' Betsy said simply.

'Who?' Gill asked, blushing hotly when her aunt pointed to the open photo album and Luke's picture. 'Did Thaddeus tell you Luke mentioned his mother to me?'

Betsy gave her a long, hard look. 'Yes.'

The brief reply wasn't encouraging, but Gill went on anyway; she had to know more. She picked the one thing puzzling her most. 'How did he come to live here with you?'

'I'm not sure it's up to me to tell you.'

Gill mentally crossed her fingers and hoped Thaddeus was right about her aunt's love of gossip.

'If Luke finds out about this he'll be mad at us both.' Betsy wagged her finger. 'I'll tell you what I know, but it's not much. There's a lot he's kept to himself.' She gave Gill a shrewd look. 'Maybe you'll be the one to winkle it out of him. He's too stoic. It's not good for him.'

'I care for him. More than I should,' Gill murmured, glancing down at her hands.

Betsy laughed. 'That's obvious, but I'm not sure about the *more than I should* part. You're a free woman and he's got no one, so what's the hitch?'

'Maybe the fact I've just been dumped by a man I thought I loved and I'm sickeningly afraid of putting myself out there again,' Gill blurted out.

'I don't blame you, but scared is no

way to live.' Betsy patted her niece's hand and then smiled. 'You'll have to ask Luke about the day we met him and thought he was Ella McBride.'

Her aunt had her complete attention now.

24

By Betsy's satisfied expression, Gill knew her aunt was enjoying this immensely.

'We'd had the inn about nine years and we were slowly renovating. We did the large room downstairs first and then started on the bedrooms. Hank was working on the Helena Suite and one day told me there must be mice in the attic, because he kept hearing scratching noises coming through the ceiling. He intended to put traps down but didn't get around to it straightaway. Then one evening he came rushing downstairs, and his face was white as that pillowcase.' She pointed over at the bed. 'He was muttering something about a voice moaning for help. I thought he'd gone loopy.'

'What was it?'

'Be patient,' Betsy admonished her. 'I

said we'd go up to the attic together. I told him there had to be a sensible explanation; but Hank was a southerner, and they tend to have a superstitious streak and relish their gothic horror stories.'

It was hard for Gill to imagine her career military uncle believing in the legend of Ella McBride, but she held her tongue.

'He insisted on going up the ladder first because he didn't want *it* to get me,' Betsy said with a chuckle. 'He opened the trapdoor as if the Hound of the Baskervilles was going to leap out at him. Instead, this thin teenage boy with bright green cat's eyes stared down at us and then asked who the heck we were.' She smiled and her eyes misted over, obviously seeing things as clearly as if they happened yesterday. 'He should have been the one afraid, but instead we both stumbled back down the ladder and Hank landed on top of me.'

Gill listened, entranced, as her aunt

continued. Apparently Luke had been hiding in the attic for several days. He'd walked and hitchhiked from Texas after running away from his last foster home, and ended up in Walland when he got a lift with a driver going to Gatlinburg for Christmas. Hanging around the town, he spotted the inn, and saw Betsy and Hank leave to go shopping. He found an open door at the back and crept in out of the cold, hoping to steal some food. After eating his fill, he'd gone exploring and found the attic.

'The little devil decided it'd make a good place to hide out, so he pinched a couple of blankets and a pillow from the laundry closet and got a bagful of food and made himself a camp in the attic,' Betsy said with admiration. 'The trouble was, we hadn't got around to flooring it completely, and he was walking from one side to the other and balancing on one of the rafters when he slipped, turning his ankle. That was the moaning Hank heard.'

Gill laughed. 'No Ella after all?'

'No, just one scrawny sixteen-year-old boy, scared of his own shadow but bound and determined not to show it. He was pitiful.' Betsy choked on her words. 'We couldn't have kids ourselves, but I've never understood how anyone can deliberately hurt one.'

'What happened to him before he got here?' Gill asked.

'He never told me the details, but some things you don't need to know, if you get what I mean. He did say he'd been shuffled between a lot of different foster homes, and I think he couldn't take it anymore.'

Gill's heart broke for him, but if she went to him now she wouldn't be able to hide what she knew, and that would be unforgiveable. It would strip away the only thing he'd clung on to all these years — his iron self-discipline. That had got him through his worst times and provided a mask between himself and a world that had treated him badly.

'You took him in and saved him.'

'I don't know about that,' Betsy said

with a shrug, 'but we gave him a home. Couldn't do otherwise.'

But they could have done, and plenty of people would. Others would have called the police and charged him with breaking and entering and stealing. Not her kind aunt and uncle though, and if she hadn't loved them before, Gill certainly did now.

'We got him into high school. Of course he was way behind, but with a bit of help we got him through.'

Gill knew there must have been a lot of heartache and struggle involved, but her aunt made what they'd done sound like nothing. 'You sent him to college too. I saw the photos.'

'Yep. Hank was so proud of the boy that day, I thought he'd burst,' Betsy said and rested her head back against the sofa, suddenly looking pale and drawn.

Gill touched her arm. 'I'm tiring you out.'

'Oh, maybe, but don't fret,' she said firmly, playing with the edge of the cushion. 'I spoke to your mum earlier.'

The swift change of subject took Gill by surprise and she didn't quite know what to say.

'We're done talking about Luke for now, my dear. Anything else you want to know, he must tell you himself. He'd string me up if he found out I'd blabbed this much.' She smiled and carried straight on. 'As for your mother, we had a good old chat. Yes, I told her I'm ill, but not that the doctors don't hold out much hope. My theory is we all have to go sometime, and I'm not sure I'm ready just yet. After I lost Hank, I didn't much care, and turned down several treatment options.'

'And now?' Gill interrupted.

'I'm reconsidering. Let's say that life seems a little more worth hanging on to these days.' A hint of colour warmed her cheeks.

Bingo. Gill had been right: there was something between her aunt and Mr Walton. If it cheered them both up and gave Betsy something to fight for, she was all for it, and was sure Uncle Hank would have been too. She reached over to give her aunt a big hug. 'I'm thrilled. I won't snoop, but whatever has changed your mind, I'm on your side.'

Betsy scoffed. 'As if you don't know, you little minx.'

Gill tried really hard to keep from smirking but lost the battle. 'My lips are sealed.'

'They had better be.'

'I believe it's time you took a nap,' Gill pronounced in her best teacher's voice. 'I'm not particularly tired anymore, so I'll leave you alone. I think I might go and read out by the fire.' She glanced down over her motley collection of garments and sighed. 'Would you prefer me to change? I don't want to offend your guests.'

'Don't be daft,' Betsy laughed. 'It's Christmas Day. You deserve a break.'

A break? Gill appreciated the irony of her aunt's comment. It was exactly what she'd come here for, but it was turning out to be the last thing she was getting. 'Right, well I'll leave you to it. Is there anything you need before I go?'

'Not a thing. Off with you.' Betsy shooed her away.

Gill picked up her book to take with her only because that was what she'd announced as her intention. The truth was that all she craved was an hour's peace to process everything her aunt had revealed.

She crept down the hallway and purposely held back when she got within sight of the large gathering room, and slowly let out the breath she'd been holding when she saw it was empty. The candles in the hurricane lamps on the mantelpiece had been lit, bathing the room in a subtle golden glow and providing the only illumination apart from the Christmas tree. She sneaked over to the closest sofa and curled up on one end, wrapping one of the soft red wool throws around her shoulders.

The only sounds came from the gently crackling fire, the antique clock marking the time, and her own steady heartbeat. The combination soothed Gill beyond belief, and for the first time in ages she truly relaxed. Her intention to do some hard thinking faded along with her eyes' desire to stay open.

'Those bunnies sure are well-behaved today.' Luke's warm chuckle sneaked into her awareness and Gill struggled to sit upright. She rubbed her tired eyes and made out the sight of Luke stretched out on the other sofa, watching her with obvious amusement.

'What do you think you're doing spying on me like this?' Gill attempted to smooth down her hair, because she didn't need a mirror to tell her it was all mussed up and standing on end.

'Spying?' His enticing drawl deepened and his gaze darkened as he continued to study her. He drank from the glass of amber liquid in his hand, then set it down on the table in front of him. 'As far as I'm aware, this is a public room, and as I've got some time off, I thought I was entitled to sit down for a while.'

'I didn't exactly mean that.' She pulled the blanket closer in around her. 'You startled me, that's all.'

'I thought you were still taking a nap to recover from the throbbing headache you'd apparently acquired after knocking back all that wine at lunch. What was it — all of maybe half a glass?' he persisted, and a rush of heat rose up her neck to flush her face. 'Was it the company you needed a rest from?'

She shrugged but didn't answer. It was too complicated.

'I'll go away and leave you alone if you prefer,' he offered.

'You're fine where you are.' *More than fine. I could look at you all day and be content.*

'Can I fix you a drink?' he offered. 'How about a drop of good Tennessee bourbon?'

'I'm not sure I should risk another hangover,' Gill teased, and a slow smile crept across his face.

'Go on, risk it and live dangerously.'

It *would* be dangerous, too. She'd

known that from the first moment they met at the airport. This strange connection that kept pulling and pushing at them was never going to be resolved if they couldn't get past the reluctance on both their parts to talk and be open with each other. One of them would have to take the chance, and Gill had the feeling many Christmases could go by before Luke Sawyer would ever take the plunge. It was up to her.

25

'I hear you were once mistaken for Ella McBride?' Gill hoped the touch of humour in her question might soften him up.

Luke didn't speak, only got up to walk over to the dresser where they kept the drinks. He kept his back to her while he topped up his own glass and poured one for her. 'I should have known you'd winkle it out of Betsy. She's always been an inveterate gossip.' His voice couldn't hide the sense of loving indulgence he had where Gill's aunt was concerned. Coming back across the room, he set her glass down on the table with a touch more force than necessary. 'Here you go. Try that.'

She took a cautious sip and choked on the fiery liquid. 'Wow. That's strong.'

'I added a touch of water,' he said with obvious amusement. 'Not much of a drinker, are you?'

'Not really. The occasional glass of wine about covers it.'

'I'm not, either. You can blame my occasional indulgence in a shot of good old Jack Daniels on Hank. He introduced me to it on my twenty-first birthday. Said if I was old enough to drink, he wanted to make sure I learned to appreciate a decent bourbon,' he explained with a smile laden with happy memories.

Gill took another small swallow. 'It's growing on me. There's a mellow, smoky taste when you get past the heat.'

'Maybe there's hope for you yet,' Luke quipped.

An easy silence fell between them, and Gill almost hated to spoil the moment. 'I understand much better now why you're so loyal to her,' she said quietly. 'Aunt Betsy hinted at how you ended up here in the first place.' Silently she pleaded with him to take a chance too. She'd made the first move and needed him to respond.

Luke's hand tightened on the glass and he sat up, leaning forward until she could almost have reached over and touched him. 'She only knows what I told them. It was the truth, just not all of it.' His raspy voice betrayed his ragged emotions, and Gill almost told him they didn't need to do this. 'I spent my first five years in a children's home. Don't ask why I never got adopted. Maybe I wasn't cute enough. Slipped through the cracks, I guess.' The blunt explanation was laced through with bitterness, and there was nothing Gill could say.

Suddenly he jumped up and crossed over to the fireplace, resting a hand on the mantel and staring into the flames. 'Then they tried foster homes in the hope one would take and they'd want to make it permanent. It didn't happen. By then I was a silent, bad-tempered kid and wouldn't let anyone get close.' He glanced around, and the fierce pain in his eyes tore at her. 'Aw, heck, don't cry.' He hurried back and dropped to his knees in front of her, wiping away the tears she hadn't even known she was shedding.

She rested her hand on his cheek. 'I don't understand how they couldn't see past the front you put on and love you.' The words tumbled out before she could bite them back.

'Oh, Gillian,' he said with a heavy sigh. 'Everyone isn't you.'

'Betsy hinted you'd been . . . hurt by some of the people you lived with.'

'Yeah, you could say that. I honestly don't want to go into details now. Betsy got me talking to a therapist and I've pretty much worked through it,' he tried to explain. 'They weren't all bad people, I promise. But by the time I was fifteen I'd been in ten different foster homes and the same number of schools. I was pretty wild.'

Gill found it hard to imagine this ultra-responsible, caring man as a rebellious teenager, but didn't try to argue.

'I started running away, and every

time the police would bring me back.'
He played idly with her hair. 'The last
time they didn't bother. They let me go.
I'd just turned sixteen. I don't blame
them; they'd had enough.'

Very gently she leaned in and pressed
a soft kiss on his mouth. 'Thank
goodness you came here.' He wrapped
his arms around her and she rested
against his broad, warm chest.

'Yeah.' He rubbed one hand in
soothing circles on her back. 'Sometimes miracles happen.'

'They certainly do,' she murmured
half to herself.

'What's happening here?' he asked,
pulling back slightly to stare into her.
'I'm bad with relationships, Gill. I
always mess up.'

'You never did with Betsy and Hank.'

'That's different,' he protested, but
she silenced him with another kiss.

'No, it's not. If you can love them for
all these years, you can do the same
with the right woman.'

'How can you be so sure?' She heard

his unspoken words and wanted to resent them. He knew just enough about her relationship with Michael to question her certainty, and she couldn't blame him. She remembered Betsy's words: *Scared is no way to live.*

'Are you willing to give it a try and see what happens, if I am?' she plunged in. What did she have to lose? 'I'll tell you anything you want to know about Michael another day.'

'What about Harry?'

'Harry? Oh, Luke, you can't be serious. He's a serial flirt. The moment any woman was silly enough to take him seriously, I'm sure he'd run a mile.' She picked her next words carefully. 'We're friends in an odd sort of way. Can you be all right with that?'

'Okay.'

'What was that an okay to?' Gill asked.

'Everything, I guess.' Luke's laconic reply took her aback, but he instantly tightened his hold on her and proceeded to draw her into one of the kisses she could never resist, and didn't want to anymore. He pulled her down into his lap and she snuggled into his warmth, knowing she'd never felt as secure and cared for in her life. Right now she didn't care about tomorrow or next week. Today was enough.

'Did it occur to you we have to feed these people again tonight?' Luke whispered, then nibbled teasing kisses all the way down her neck.

'Spoilsport,' Gill grouched.

'Ah, but remember how much you enjoy watching me in the kitchen,' he teased.

'I don't think I'm cut out for inn-keeping.'

He tipped a finger to her chin so she had to look at him. 'You're a natural at the whole people thing, plus you wield a mean duster and vacuum.'

'I'm so glad I've impressed you with my cleaning skills. I've never thought of it in terms of a flirting technique before,' she joked. 'But whatever works, I suppose.'

He bent down to take hold of her

feet. 'It's the bunny slippers really. Forget Dior dresses and thousand-dollar designer shoes. Those pink fluffy tails do it for me every time.'

'Pervert!' Gill shrieked as he wriggled his fingers inside to tickle the soles of her feet. 'Stop!'

'Only if you beg me,' he teased, but suddenly let go and clung to her, burying his face in her hair.

'What's wrong?' she whispered, and shifted so she could see him properly. The good humour that had been lighting up his face had been replaced by confusion.

'You make me laugh, a lot, and I'm not used to that. It's not who I usually am,' he tried to explain. 'There wasn't a lot of fun in my life growing up, and by the time I got here I was kind of set in my ways. Betsy and Hank tried to get me to lighten up, but I couldn't stand the thought of letting them down, so I never let up on myself.'

Gill picked up his hands, rubbing her fingers over the rough calluses and making him shiver at her touch. 'You were afraid they'd send you away, the same as everyone else had.'

'I guess,' Luke reluctantly agreed. 'With your close family it must be hard for you to understand.'

She nodded. 'But I want to try. It all comes down to trust in the end.' She left the thought hanging out there and didn't say anything more, just snuggled back into his warm arms.

'It's not going to happen overnight,' he murmured.

'Good. I'm not ready to rush into anything.' The last thing she needed was to commit herself to anything with this complex man before they took their time to find out more about each other. She'd thought she knew Michael, but had made a huge mistake, and her heart couldn't take another battering.

Luke drew them into a wonderful, sweet kiss and she gave up thinking too hard. 'Do you want to watch me make turkey tortilla soup with the leftovers from lunch?'

'You certainly know how to woo a woman,' Gill said with a mocking laugh. 'Is that how you win over all the girls?'

'I understand you're teasing, but I have a hard job playing those kinds of games.' He sounded sad. 'Maybe it's why I've always failed with women. If you want that sort of man, you're on the wrong track. I'm straightforward because I don't know how to be any other way.'

'That's fine, but remember there's nothing wrong with having a sense of humour. I know you're not completely a lost cause because of your predilection for bunny slippers.'

He tossed up his hands in the air. 'You got me there. Guilty as charged.'

'Come and amaze me with your soup-making skills,' she ordered with a laugh, and he joined in, proving he wasn't a lost cause. She always enjoyed a challenge.

26

'Please tell me the latest weather forecast is more encouraging,' Portia pleaded as she played with a slice of crusty bread, reducing it to crumbs with her fingers.

They were gathered around the dining table having supper, and to Gill's relief everyone seemed a lot more mellow than earlier in the day. The conversation had flowed easily between an exciting new movie Helen had seen recently and Thaddeus's enthusiastic description of the last hike he had taken before his accident.

'It is,' Luke said succinctly, and Gill fixed a brief, hard stare on him. *She wants more than that, you idiot*. His skin flushed and he hurried on. 'The storm should go north of us and we'll be above freezing by morning, so will start thawing out. I heard the ploughs will make it out here first thing.'

Harry tossed another handful of crispy tortilla chips into his soup bowl. 'I checked with the Knoxville airport, and they're hopeful the New York flight will get out of there tomorrow afternoon.' He scooped up a big spoonful and began to eat. 'This is delicious. You're a — '

'Why didn't you say?' Portia interrupted. 'You can be a very annoying man.'

'Good thing you've known me long enough not to be bothered, isn't it, sweetheart?' Harry's wry comment made Gill almost choke on a mouthful of soup. 'I had business plans to make.'

'Your father isn't a slave driver — I'm sure he's not working you hard over the holidays,' Portia retorted. 'Don't try to tell me you're sailing either, not in the dead of winter, unless you're jetting off to the Caribbean.'

'I do have other irons in the fire,' Harry replied, glancing over at Gill, who wished he wouldn't draw attention to her.

Luke reached over and picked up her hand from the table, cradling it in his own, and she tried not to smile at his unsubtle gesture of possession. 'Would anyone care for more soup?' he asked. 'I made a large pot.' Everyone declared they were full and didn't even have space for a slice of cake or pie to round off the meal. 'How about coffee?'

'Fix some for us, dear,' Betsy piped up. 'We always watch *It's a Wonderful Life* on Christmas night, so that's what I plan to do, and anyone is welcome to join me.'

Portia rolled her eyes as though she couldn't imagine anything more tedious. She made her excuses and went off to have an early night, followed closely behind by Helen.

'Thanks for the offer, but I've some work to do, contrary to my friends' belief,' Harry said, giving them all a friendly smile before disappearing off up the stairs.

'We'd be happy to watch, wouldn't we, Gill?' Luke asked. Gill felt absurdly pleased at the casual way he said 'we' and nodded her agreement. There were far worse ways to spend a cold wintery evening than cuddled up with her favourite man on a large squishy sofa in the dark.

'Do you want to dress up and go outside for a few minutes? The sky's real clear tonight so the stars should be spectacular,' Luke suggested when they were finally alone again.

The four of them had watched the gloriously sentimental film and then finished off the evening with hot cocoa. Thaddeus had taken a yawning but happy Betsy off so they could both get to bed. He'd mentioned possibly leaving himself, as he thought his arm was well enough for him to drive, but Betsy told him not to talk nonsense. She almost ordered him to stay until at least the New Year and he'd easily capitulated.

'I'd love to.' Gill sighed with contentment. 'You know I'd expected to merely tolerate Christmas this year, but it's turned into something special.'

Luke wrapped her in his arms and pressed a soft kiss on her mouth. 'It certainly has.' His eyes gleamed. 'I hate to admit this, but I need to if I'm really trying to get better at the honesty thing. I tried to persuade your aunt not to invite you here while she was gone.'

'Why?' Gill said, taken aback by his startling admission.

'I knew she needed a break, but I told her I could manage perfectly well on my own.' He glanced down and then back up at her again. 'She'd mentioned your broken engagement, and I didn't want to have to deal with an over-emotional woman crying all the time. Plus I guessed you wouldn't know anything about the business but would think you were in charge and try to order me around.' He looked completely shamefaced, and Gill considered whether to tear him off a strip or take pity on him.

He deserved to suffer a bit. 'Charming, I'm sure,' she declared, and watched him flinch. 'You weren't the only apprehensive one.' Luke's dark eyebrows rose but he didn't say a word. 'I was so relieved when I thought the safe-looking older man at the airport with the braces and checked shirt was going to be the hotel handyman. When you introduced yourself I hated the fact I immediately fancied you, because I wasn't supposed to be attracted to any man for a very long time.' Luke's mouth curved up at the corners and Gill sensed him trying not to smile.

'I haven't dated anyone properly in years, Gill, because the last time was a disaster. The day you arrived I wasn't exactly looking to be bowled over either,' he said with a grimace.

'And were you?' She gave him a coy glance from under her eyelashes.

'Was I what?'

'Bowled over,' she whispered into the side of his neck as she sneaked a quick kiss.

He grasped her shoulders and pulled back so she couldn't avoid the sight of his flushed face. 'Yes. Satisfied now?'

'I do believe I am,' Gill purred. 'You know, I think we're getting the hang of flirting.'

His large, sure hands slid down around her waist and he pulled her closer. 'You'd tempt a saint to flirt.'

'What a thing to say to me,' she declared with mock indignation. 'How about this walk we were going to take? A little cooling down might be good for both of us.'

'You could stick me in a freezer and I'd still want you,' Luke mused. 'Okay. Get your coat and we'll go out and shiver together.'

She ran off, humming to herself, and let herself quietly into the bedroom.

'Tired, are you?' Betsy piped up from her bed, raising up and turning her light back on.

'I'm surprised you're still awake. We're just going outside to admire the stars,' Gill explained, aware how weak it sounded.

Betsy frowned. 'Be careful.'

Gill didn't understand what her aunt

was getting at. One minute she was practically throwing her at Luke, and now she appeared to be warning her off.

'I don't want my boy hurt.'

'Why would I do that?' Gill asked.

'Because you're only here for another week and then you'll be off back to Cornwall.' Betsy sighed. 'I've never seen him this way before.'

Gill sat on the arm of the sofa and thought carefully before she spoke again. 'I thought you wanted Luke to be more open to life?'

'I do, but . . . ' Betsy's breath hitched in a sob and Gill hurried over to sit on the bed, pulling her aunt into her arms.

'Shush. Don't upset yourself,' she pleaded. 'We're both cautious for our own reasons. There's no way we'll be rushing into anything.' Managing to sound logical and sensible now wasn't hard, but Gill suspected as soon as she set eyes on Luke again that it would all fly out of the window. 'Try to be happy for us.'

Betsy gently pulled away and wiped at her eyes. 'I am, really. Hank always said I worried too much.'

Changing the subject seemed smart. 'Did I hear you persuading a certain gentleman to stay a while longer?' Her aunt's cheeks turned bright pink and she nodded. 'Good. Now I'm going out for a while. You get some sleep. Please.' Betsy pretended to agree, but Gill knew only too well she wouldn't rest until her niece was tucked up in the pull-out bed.

She slid off the bed and went on a search for her boots. Retrieving them from under the table, she tugged them on and added her puffy coat and a pair of wool gloves. Luke would think she'd changed her mind if she took any longer.

Gill hurried back down the hallway and into the gathering room, but skidded to a halt as the two men standing together over by the fireplace turned to stare at her.

'There you are.' Luke's emotionless

voice was chilling. The warm smile was gone, replaced by barely controlled anger. 'Harry came looking for you.'

'Oh, right.' Gill's heart thumped in her chest. 'What do you need?' She turned her attention to the other man.

'Apparently he hoped you'd been able to get hold of a certain necklace you'd discussed with him,' Luke replied before Harry could speak. 'I believe it's in connection with tracking down the biological mother of a 'friend' of yours.' He spelled it all out with clinical precision and stood, arms folded in front of his chest, his emerald eyes boring into her.

Harry glanced awkwardly between the two of them and Gill watched the penny drop.

27

'I'll say good night to you both,' Luke announced with such excruciating politeness Gill wanted to scream.

'Stay. Please. I'm sorry. This is all my fault,' Gill tried to apologize, but in the flickering shadows from the fire his face turned to stone. She understood it was the only way he knew to retain control, but longed to throw her arms around him and plead for his forgiveness.

'Yes, it is. I'm sure in your own way you meant well. Obviously I made an unwise choice discussing this subject with you in the first place, but that was my mistake.' He angled his head to nod at Harry. 'I'd appreciate it very much if you would abandon this foolish search. I have no interest in the result.'

'Uh, yeah, sure thing,' Harry mumbled.

'I've locked up the front door and I'll see to the back one on my way out.

Maybe you can see to the fire when you're done here and plan breakfast for once.' The borderline rudeness was so unlike him that Gill cringed.

'Of course.' She bit her tongue as he strode off without another word. In the horrid silence she heard the back door slam shut.

Harry gently touched her arm. 'Come here.' He led her over to the sofa and pushed her to sit down before joining her. 'I screwed up. Sorry. It never occurred to me you were talking about Mr Sawyer.'

'There's no reason why it should have,' Gill whispered through the tears rolling helplessly down her cheeks. She made a hopeless effort to brush them away but gave up and dissolved into loud wrenching sobs.

'I've already made some enquiries and was following up a couple of possible leads. Do you want me to keep looking?' he asked, holding out a clean white handkerchief.

Gill took it and dabbed at her swollen

eyes. She must look a sight, but couldn't bring herself to care. 'I'm not sure.'

'Think about it and give me your decision in the morning.' He gave her a kind smile. 'If it helps at all, most people want to know, even if they deny it.'

'Thanks.' She pulled herself back up to standing. 'I'm sorry you got mixed up in this. I had this fantasy of presenting Luke with the report you'd done with all his mother's details and him throwing his arms around me and thanking me before rushing off to get in touch with her.'

'And then you'd live happily ever after?' Harry's cynicism cut through her fantasy and Gill knew that was all it had ever been. 'Unfortunately it doesn't usually work that way. In a few rare cases the people connect, but mostly there's too much resentment and guilt for them to get past. Doesn't mean they're sorry they did it, though.'

Gill nodded. 'I'll sleep on it.' But that

was a stupid thing to say, because she surely wouldn't sleep a wink tonight. 'I've got to dampen down the fire and sort out some things in the kitchen. I'll see you at breakfast and let you know about continuing the search or not.'

'Are you sure you'll be all right on your own?' Harry said with a frown.

'Fine.' She put back on her best professional smile. 'I'm sharing a room with my aunt, so I won't have time to brood.'

'Okay. Take care. You're a good girl. He'll thank you one day,' Harry declared, gave her a quick kiss on the forehead, and headed towards the stairs.

I'm not so sure. I might have just ruined the best thing to ever happen to me.

Gill sank back down on the sofa with her head in her hands and cried until she was certain her heart would break. Then she told herself not to be stupid. It already had broken.

★ ★ ★

In the early-morning darkness she crept around as quietly as possible and managed to make it all the way to the bedroom door.

'You're up early, Gillian. Did you sleep well?' Betsy asked.

She had no choice but to turn back around and put on a smile. 'Not too bad.' She refused to burden her aunt with her problems. Anyway, she'd been worried about Gill and Luke getting serious last night, so from that point of view she might even be pleased. 'I need to go and see to breakfast. Would you like me to bring you some later?'

'Don't worry about me. I'm sure Thaddeus will see to it and join me. We do enjoy our quiet breakfasts together,' Betsy said with an enigmatic smile.

Gill nodded. 'Good.' Before she could be interrogated about what the stars looked like last night, she made her escape. *Please let Luke not be in the kitchen already.* She desperately needed to get things organized, and herself under some sort of control, before facing Luke and his angry resentment again.

The moment she opened the swing door Gill saw her prayer hadn't been answered.

'Coffee's ready. The oven's hot and the tables are laid.' Luke's unemotional recitation made her eyes fill with tears, but she fought them back down. He kept his back to her while he cut up fruit and arranged it on the platter she'd placed out on the counter last night.

'Thank you,' she replied, equally stiff and unyielding. This was plainly the only way they would be with each other now. It was going to be a long ten days unless she considered changing her plane ticket to fly back home early.

Without speaking any more than necessary, they somehow got breakfast ready. Gill started to carry the food out to place on warming trays on the table ready for the guests to help themselves.

Harry appeared by her right shoulder, startling her. 'Good morning.'

'Oh, it's you.'

He gave her bemused look. 'You sure don't puff up a man's ego. Maybe next time you could try to sound more enthusiastic.'

She tried to respond to his joke but a laugh died in her throat. 'Sorry.'

'It's okay, kid.' He touched her face. 'Who didn't get any sleep?'

No makeup had been effective enough to conceal the vicious dark circles under her eyes or the grey sheen to her skin, but having the fact pointed out didn't boost her ego either.

Harry glanced around and then leaned in closer, lowering his voice. 'Did you decide whether you want me to keep searching for Luke's mother?'

Until he asked, Gill had been going backwards and forwards around her head trying to make up her mind, but in one second she knew her answer. 'Yes, and I know it could be impossible without the necklace but I still want you to try. Whatever was between me and Luke is over, but I still care for him

274

and he needs this to move on properly with his life.' Putting her thoughts into words helped, and the knot of tension in her stomach eased slightly for the first time since last night's disaster.

A sly smile lit up Harry's face. 'He's lucky to have you. I wish he realized it, but we men are dumb sometimes.'

'Only sometimes?' Gill tossed back at him.

'Hey, I'm trying to help you here.' He threw up his hands in surrender.

'Sorry.' A rush of embarrassment flushed her face and neck.

Harry gently wrapped an arm around her shoulders. 'Don't be such a worrier. I'm not going to be offended by a touch of sarcasm thrown in my direction. If I was, I'd have keeled over long ago.'

His easy humour briefly made Gill wish she could fancy him instead. A light flirtation and casual goodbye would have suited them both. Instead she had to fall hard for a challenging, difficult man with the self-control of a block of granite.

'I've got an idea,' he declared with a satisfied grin.

'Do I even want to hear?' Gill jibed back at him, afraid what he might come up with next.

'I could be offended, but I'll chose not to be,' he said in a fake pompous voice that finally dragged a smile out of her. 'I'm a darn good artist, though I say it myself. If you come to my room after breakfast, you can describe the necklace and I'll draw it. Consider it a jewellery photo-fit session.'

To Gill the idea sounded highly unlikely to succeed, but she didn't want to burst his bubble. 'I suppose we could give it a go.'

'Don't be too enthusiastic,' he protested with a smile.

'I won't.' She glanced at the table and remembered what she was supposed to be doing. 'I must go and get the coffee or I'll be told off again.' She tried to make light of it, but the words caught in her throat.

Harry rested his hands on her

shoulders. 'You're a strong woman. Don't let Sawyer get to you. He's got issues and refuses to face up to them, which isn't your fault. You've tried to help and he's chosen to reject the offer.'

Something about his innate confidence seeped into Gill's bloodstream, and she straightened up. 'Thanks.'

'What for?' he asked, giving her a puzzled frown.

'Helping me see the situation more clearly.' She stared deep into his clear blue eyes. 'You're a good man who for some reason likes to pretend he isn't. I'm off to face the lion in his den again. Wish me luck!' She turned away and marched towards the kitchen.

28

Gill stopped at the sight of her aunt busily making a pot of tea and Thaddeus buttering slices of toast. 'Oh, I'm surprised to see you both up already.' She glanced around the room. 'Where's Luke?'

Betsy reached into the cupboard for two mugs and then gave Gill a long, searching stare. 'He's gone out to make sure the porch and steps aren't slippery. Said he needed to clear off his truck too, and make sure it's good to run the other guests to the airport later.'

'Right.' Gill waited to see if anything else had been said.

'Luke wasn't his usual self this morning,' Thaddeus commented, and Gill felt another rush of heat flood her face. 'In fact he was quite rude when your aunt asked what was bothering him.'

'Have you any idea what might be up with him?' Betsy persisted, and frowned when Gill didn't answer. 'I warned you, didn't I?'

Her aunt's sharp voice took Gill aback. She'd started all this with the simple wish to help Luke, but now she'd alienated him along with Betsy and probably Thaddeus too. Without betraying Luke even further, she couldn't even defend herself.

'Yes you did, and I'm sorry,' Gill apologized, and started to clear away the breakfast dishes.

A few minutes later they left without saying another word, although she did catch a pitying glance from Thaddeus on his way out the door. She slumped forward, holding on to the edge of the counter and fighting back more tears.

'The girls aren't coming down to breakfast,' Harry announced as he strode in. He stopped as she looked up with tears streaming down her face. 'Have you been in here crying all this time?' His tone of voice was sad rather than accusatory.

The next thing Gill knew, she was

wrapped in his arms and weeping into his soft cashmere jumper. She tried to explain through gulping sobs, but he gently shushed her.

'You're going to leave this work until later and come up to my room. I think we need coffee, or do you prefer tea?' he asked.

'Coffee is fine. Milk but no sugar,' she murmured. He let go and found everything he was looking for, which was just as well, as she was helpless.

'Come on, kid.' He carried their two mugs and shooed her out of the kitchen and towards the stairs.

Ten minutes later she stared at him in amazement. 'That's incredible.'

'Is it close?' Harry asked, holding out the detailed pencil drawing. She'd described the necklace as best she could remember, and with a few swift strokes he'd captured it perfectly.

'You're a genius,' Gill declared, and he beamed as if she'd handed him a million dollars. 'What will you do with it now?'

'I've contacts in the jewellery world, so I'll circulate this around. It's very distinctive, and most jewellers who make personalized pieces keep good records — plus they have excellent memories.' He gave her a firm no-nonsense stare, very unlike his usual easy manner. 'This is your last chance to stop me.'

She drew in a deep breath and met his clear blue eyes head-on. 'Find out the truth. Please.'

He nodded. 'Fair enough.' He stood up and handed her their two empty coffee mugs. 'There you go. Run off and do your domestic duties. I'm going to pack and then work on this investigation until lunch. You did say one o'clock, right?'

'Yes. We'll have it ready and then Luke will take you all to the airport.' Even saying his name hurt, but she managed a smile. 'And thank you for everything.'

He opened the door and stood to one side, then suddenly touched her arm. 'I'm the one who should be thanking you.'

'Why? All I've done is cause you a lot of aggravation,' Gill said lightly.

'You gave me something of interest to do, plus you didn't pay any attention to any of my usual nonsense,' he explained, and shoved his hands in his pockets, looking incredibly awkward.

She reached up and kissed his cheek. 'Don't underestimate yourself. Remember what you told me about being strong,' she said bluntly, and immediately hurried off. On the small landing halfway down the stairs, she stopped. Luke stood with his hand on the banister rail, glaring up at her.

'I was looking for you,' he snapped. 'I suppose you were with your new best friend?'

'What's it to you?' Gill refused to give him the satisfaction of being cowed by his abrasive manner.

'Absolutely nothing.'

She met his fierce stare with one of her own and waited him out.

'Sorry. I'm being a jerk again,' he growled. She almost felt sorry for him but was determined not to let her sympathy show. He'd tossed it back in her face before, and she wasn't in the mood to go another round with him.

'All I wanted was to discuss a grocery list with you,' he added. 'I figured I'd stock up on the way back from the airport. The roads are pretty much clear now, as long as people don't go too crazy and speed.'

'Doesn't Betsy usually decide on meals? I don't want to cut her out and offend her,' Gill explained, not adding that her aunt was barely speaking to her at the moment.

'She told me to ask you.'

'Really?' It didn't make sense, but she was here to help, so had better go along with whatever her aunt wanted. Flinging them back in each other's orbit was going to be a waste of time. Gill didn't think for a moment that talking about how many loaves of bread they needed was going to break down the impenetrable wall Luke had erected between them. 'We can go into the kitchen, I suppose.' He turned and stalked off without another word, and very reluctantly she followed.

She purposely chose not to sit down. Walking around to check on things was far safer than being within touching distance of the man who'd sneaked into her heart while she wasn't looking. No matter how rude or cold he was to her, it didn't matter deep down. She still wanted to feel his lips on hers again and rest her head in the hollow of his neck, the spot perfectly sized for her to fit into. Unconsciously, she sighed and glanced back around from checking on the spaghetti to meet his penetrating gaze fixed on her.

'Why the heavy sigh?' His gruff voice ripped through her good intentions and she couldn't hold back any longer.

'I hate that you won't talk to me. I know you were shocked and upset last night, but I hoped you might have come to your senses by now.' Her exasperation poured out, and the flash of pain in his previously ice cold eyes gave her hope. 'I love you. I know I shouldn't for a ton of different reasons, least of which being the fact I'm not at all sure you know how to love me back.'

He stepped forward and seized her in his arms, then captured her mouth in his, losing them in a wonderful dizzying kiss. All she knew was that she never wanted him to stop. But finally he did, resting his cheek against her before sliding his hands down to the base of her spine and pressing them both together, so close there was no knowing where she ended and he began.

'I lashed out at you because I'm scared,' he whispered into her warm skin. 'For so long it's been at the back of mind, but it's sort of safe there.'

'I know, and you'd be odd if you weren't apprehensive,' she replied. Then she started to tell him quietly everything Harry had said. 'It usually isn't a magic pill to make everything right.'

'Does he really think there's a chance of finding her?' Luke asked.

She dare not raise his hopes too high,

because she wasn't sure he could cope with them being shattered again. 'He can't promise, but he's worked on similar cases with a lot of success.' She hastened to explain herself better. 'By success, I mean he's tracked the person down. After that it's out of his court.'

'Yeah, I understand.' Luke stroked her hair as he spoke and she shivered at his touch, needing it so badly she could hardly breathe. 'I've no reason to believe she'll even want to be contacted. She could even be . . . not around anymore.'

'But at least you would know,' Gill murmured.

He pulled back to fix her with his unflinching emerald gaze. 'Exactly. I've come to the conclusion I have to do this, or I can't move on and put this in its proper place. It's a part of my past — a large one — but I want a future, Gill.' He grasped her hands. 'Hopefully with you.'

'What are you asking?' she said in a whisper, her heart thumping loudly up against her ribs.

He stroked a finger down her cheek. 'When this is over, one way or the other, would you consider going steady?' he asked with a crooked half-smile. 'No promises on either side until we're certain of each other.'

'That sounds reasonable,' she stammered, wondering what she'd just agreed to.

'Good. You have to help me get through this first, though,' he pleaded. 'Deal?'

'Deal.' Gill smiled and mentally crossed her fingers at the same time.

29

The piles of luggage waiting by the door to be loaded made Gill smile. She thought of the modest-sized suitcase she'd brought with her and knew she'd never be in the same league as these women. It was amusing to watch them, though. Portia had already made sure Luke had stowed all her items in the back of the truck correctly, while bemoaning the fact the Mockingbird vehicle wasn't available. Being squashed in Luke's truck wasn't her idea of the proper way to travel. Helen was as laid-back as usual, sprawled elegantly on the sofa, dressed in something scarlet and low-cut in inappropriate places, considering the cold weather. Gill could feel Portia's impatience from where she stood near the fire. Her most trying guest was perched on one of the dining room chairs in her classic black

Chanel trouser suit and towering heels, continually glaring at Luke and Harry and then looking at her watch. The men were huddled together by the stairs, and it wasn't hard to guess what they were talking so intently about.

Harry touched Luke's shoulder and then headed in her direction. 'Time to go back to the wicked city,' he proclaimed. 'I bet you'll miss me.'

'Like a hole in the head, Harry, dear,' Gill retorted, and he tossed his head back, roaring with laughter.

'You're a death knell to my self-esteem,' he declared, and put on a sad face.

'You'll survive. Put one decorative lady on each arm and you'll be the most envied man at the Knoxville airport.'

'Huh,' he scoffed. 'There probably won't be much competition.' Suddenly his expression turned serious and he edged closer. 'Luke spoke to me.'

'Good.'

'Not sure what you said to him, but it must have worked,' he said with a shrug.

She skipped over a direct reply, unwilling to reveal something so private. 'Did he show you the necklace?'

'Yep. He's going to email me pictures of it, too.'

'How long do these things usually take?' she asked.

'There's no way of knowing. Some you can solve a case with a couple of phone calls. Others take months.' He hesitated. 'Then there are the rare few that elude us.'

A heavy silence fell between them, and Gill had to drag out all her reserves of strength not to crumble. She must temper her expectations, and Luke's too. Their future couldn't rest totally on Harry being successful in his search.

'I understand.'

Harry leaned in to kiss her cheek. 'I'll do my best.'

'I know you will.' She needed him to go before she couldn't hold it together any longer. 'Luke's ready to leave, I think.'

He nodded and picked up his own

bags from the floor. 'Come on, ladies, time to head back to civilization.'

A few minutes later they were gone in a swirl of perfume and goodbyes. The inn seemed strangely quiet, and Gill merely stood and enjoyed it for a while, letting the silence wrap around her.

'One step at a time, my dear,' came Thaddeus's voice by her shoulder. 'Your aunt is tired and she's lying down.' His concern shone through, and she realized that Betsy's health hadn't been the priority it should have been for her. A wave of guilt for being too wrapped up in Luke swept over her and she rushed to apologize.

'Stop that now. She'd be annoyed to hear you.' His eyes softened. 'Seeing you two happy again cheered her at lunch.' He smiled. 'Of course, I had to almost tie her down so she didn't poke her nose in and ask too many questions.'

'Did Luke tell her anything?' Gill cautiously asked, unsure how much she should or shouldn't reveal.

'Only that you have some sort of . . . understanding.'

That sounded like something straight out of a Jane Austen novel, but she supposed it described their vague arrangement as well as anything. She must keep the story about his mother to herself. Luke probably guessed it would upset Betsy, mainly because she'd hate to see him hurt any more.

'Are you still going home as planned?' Thaddeus asked.

'Of course. I've got my classes to get back to. We'll work something out.' Her voice faded away as the small amount of time they had left struck her hard.

'I'm sure you will,' he said kindly, and she only wished she could be as certain.

Saying any more would be unwise, because it would only get passed straight on to her aunt. 'I'd better get back to work. No rest for the wicked.' She smiled and hurried off towards the kitchen. With the door shut behind her, she chuckled to herself at how this room had become a refuge instead of the most feared place in the inn, as it had been only a week ago.

They had so much food left over from their Christmas lunch that she didn't need to fret about dinner tonight. She was suddenly struck with the crazy notion to follow Luke's suggestion on the day she'd arrived: *There's no better place around to drink your morning coffee, even in this chilly weather. It's worth dressing up warmly for.*

Gill wasn't sure he'd meant when there was snow on the ground, but she couldn't resist. She didn't want to disturb her aunt by going back to her room for more clothes, so she grabbed a heavy old coat Luke kept on a hook by the back door. Of course it swamped her, but she rolled up the sleeves enough to reveal her hands. Then she walked back out into the main room and picked up a couple of the wool throws lying on the back of the sofa. Hot coffee would be nice, but she couldn't juggle anything else.

As she opened the front door, the frigid air hit her and her resolve wobbled. She selected a chair right in the middle of the row with the best view of the river, and used the small brush her aunt kept out there to sweep the snow off the seat. Tucking her feet up, she made herself as comfortable as possible, wrapping one of the blankets around her head and shoulders and the other over her legs.

She managed to get the chair rocking slowly and started to truly admire the beautiful view. The snow-draped trees sparkled in the afternoon sunshine and the river bubbled gently along in front of her, infusing her with a sense of peace she hadn't felt in a long time. She let herself imagine what it would be like to watch the changing seasons from this very spot. For the longest time she did nothing but think.

'You took me seriously, didn't you?' Luke's jocular voice startled her from her reflections. 'I didn't mean you had to freeze to death in the process.' He watched her from the steps, shaking his head in dismay.

'I didn't hear you come back.'

'Probably because your ears have turned to ice.' He came over to stand in front of her and tugged off his heavy leather gloves. Next he slipped his warm hands under her makeshift head covering to cradle her face. 'God, woman, you need to get inside before you catch your death.'

'Coming from a man stupid enough to barbeque steaks when it's below freezing, that's rich,' she tossed back at him, unable to stop herself laughing.

'Will the promise of the best hot chocolate ever tempt you to abandon your post?'

She pretended to consider the offer. 'It might.'

'Good.' Before she could say another word, he scooped her up off the chair and headed for the door.

'You're mad,' she protested, tightening her arms around his neck to stop from falling, although his hold was tight enough that she wasn't going anywhere.

Once inside, he stopped to wipe his feet and let her slide back down to the ground, then unwound the blankets and tossed them aside. 'Go over by the fire and warm up while I fix our drinks.'

'Thanks.' Gill popped a kiss on his cheek and happily ran over to stand in front of the fireplace to thaw out while he disappeared off towards the kitchen. She held her hands out to warm up, and then the change in temperature made her nose start to run. She fumbled in the pockets of Luke's coat for a handkerchief and pulled out a handful of stuff: old receipts, a comb, and some random scraps of paper; but not a tissue in sight. She was about to shove it all back in when a crumpled business card caught her eye. She straightened it out and read it, then read it again.

Luke strolled back in, beaming happily at her. 'Here we go, hot chocolate with an excess of marshmallows. That should unfreeze you.'

She didn't answer immediately, or make any move to take the large mug he was holding out to her.

'What's up?' he asked, and she held out the card to him.

'Don't you think letting me believe you're a simple handyman who happens to be a pretty good cook was rather misleading?' Her acerbic manner wiped the smile from his face.

30

'Did I ever say that?' Luke challenged.

'It was implied, and you let me believe it.' Gill started to read from the card. 'Luke Sawyer. Hospitality and Customer Service Instructor. Culinary Institute of America. St Helena, CA.'

Luke set the mugs down on the table and closed the gap between them, resting his large hands on her shoulders so she couldn't have moved even if she wanted to. 'I'm sorry you feel I misled you. It wasn't intentional. There never seemed to be the right moment without having you think I was boasting or making you feel small.' The rasp in his voice got to her and she blinked back tears. 'You may not believe this, but from day one I wanted you to think the best of me, but . . . '

'I'm sorry too. I overreacted,' Gill conceded. 'How about we drink our hot chocolate and then talk?'

'Good plan, kiddo. Come on.' He gently pushed her towards the sofa and encouraged her to sit, then passed her one of the large stoneware mugs and settled down to join her.

For a few minutes they companionably enjoyed the richly flavoured drinks that didn't even begin to resemble any of the packet mixes Gill had grown up with, and warmed themselves up by the fire. Then Luke took her empty mug and set it down by his own, before sliding his arm around her shoulders and easing her back against his chest. Without any prompting, he quietly started to tell her his story. He'd become interested in cooking and the hotel business from being around Betsy and Hank at the inn. They'd encouraged him to follow his passion, and he'd got his Culinary Arts Management degree from the Culinary Institute of America, as stated on his card.

'I worked a few years in various restaurants and a New York hotel, and then had the chance to return to California as an instructor at the St Helena campus,' he explained. 'I enjoyed teaching and sharing my passion with the students.'

'I completely understand that. There's nothing more rewarding than when you see the lightbulb come on.' She decided to ask the next question even though she was pretty sure she knew the answer. 'Why did you quit?'

His eyes darkened. 'Why do you think? Betsy wasn't well even before Hank passed away, but when I came back for his funeral I realized quite how ill she was, and it was obvious she wouldn't be able to run the inn herself. It didn't occur to me to do anything other than stay.'

Gill smiled, certain now that she hadn't made another mistake in trusting this man. He would never lead her on the way Michael had done and then betray her. Luke didn't know how to be anything other than honourable. 'You're a good man.'

'I try.' His simple statement got to her more than any more flowery reply would have done. 'I'll always tell it like it is, Gill, whether it's what you want to hear or not. I can't be any different.'

'Good.' She wrapped her arms around his neck and pulled him to her for a long, delicious kiss. Reluctantly, she let go and sighed. 'I expect you want to know more about Michael.'

He gave her a considering glance, then took hold of her hands and stared deep into her eyes. 'I think you need to tell me for your own sake.'

Of course he was right, but that didn't make it any easier. Gill took a deep breath and ploughed straight on before she could lose her nerve. As she went through the whole story, Luke's kind, interested expression never altered.

'So, that's it, really,' she concluded. 'Coming here was the best thing I could have done,' she added with a smile, 'and that doesn't take into account meeting you. It's given me the mental and physical distance to see everything more clearly.'

'So no fancy dresses and horse-drawn carriages next time?' he said with a wicked gleam in his eyes.

'I didn't say that,' she protested, and then smacked him on the arm when he laughed out loud. Suddenly they both went very quiet, and held on tightly to each other.

'What going to happen with us?' Gill whispered, nuzzling into the warm skin exposed by Luke's open-necked shirt.

He stroked a hand down over her hair, and his soothing fingers eased something inside her. 'I think we're goin' to get to know each other better. Pay a few visits back and forth across the Atlantic. And then maybe, hopefully, we'll want to be together long-term. I don't have much practice at the whole romance thing, but I'll sure as heck try. You good with that?'

She kissed him again, deciding that could do the answering for her.

'Gillian Elizabeth! Whatever are you doing?'

Gill jerked around and met her

mother's horrified face. She'd heard the expression 'struck dumb' many times before, but had never experienced it quite so literally. She sensed Luke shift next to her, and next thing he was on his feet and holding out his hand to her mother.

'Luke Sawyer. You must be Mrs. Robinson. I can see the resemblance.' He flashed one of the charming smiles that had won Gill over from the beginning. But by the way her mother's stony face didn't alter, she took a wild guess it wasn't having the same effect on her.

'Are you the boy Betsy took in?' Patricia asked in a no-nonsense tone, surprising Gill, who'd never heard it mentioned before.

'Yep, that would be me,' he said quietly.

'I thought you left a long time ago.'

Gill flinched at her mother's blunt manner, but Luke never wavered. 'I came back when Hank got sick. I work here now.'

Finally Gill got her senses back enough to properly register what was going on. She glanced behind her mother and gave a shriek. 'Daddy!' Jumping up, she flung herself at them both, and then they were all hugging each other.

'Your mother wouldn't rest after she heard about poor Betsy,' her dad explained, and Gill's mind raced.

'But what about your heart?' she asked her mother, frowning and worried now. 'I hope you haven't put your health at risk.'

'I'm not stupid,' Patricia retorted. 'I checked with the doctor, and he said I should be fine as long as I'm careful not to overdo it and take my medicine as he instructed. Your father organized a wheelchair for me at the airports, so that helped.' She gave Luke a long, hard stare. 'Of course, arriving to find you kissing a man you haven't even told me about has caused me added stress.'

'I did mention him!' Gill protested.

'Only as the handyman who worked

around the inn. I thought you were still heartbroken.'

A rush of heat lit up Gill's face at her mother's sharp comment, and she caught sight of Luke's obvious amusement. He moved closer and slid his arm around her waist, pulling her to him and giving her a reassuring squeeze.

'I'm pleased to say the Long River Inn has worked its magic yet again.' Luke offered the explanation along with a broad grin. 'Would you like me to let Betsy know you're here?'

Gill could have kissed him again. He knew they needed a few moments alone.

'That's very kind of you,' Patricia said with a stiff nod.

Luke leaned down to whisper in Gill's ear. 'Don't worry if we don't return right away. She might be taking a nap, and I'm guessing she'll want to smarten up before coming out.'

His kindness tugged at Gill's heart and, if she hadn't acknowledged it before, she knew now how much she loved him. He left them and she turned back to face her parents.

'Why don't you come and sit down? Luke will see to your bags later. Would you like a cup of tea?' she babbled.

'We'll sit, but I want to talk while we have the chance. Tea can wait,' her mother ordered, and she had no choice but to obey.

'You're looking well,' her father spoke up.

'I'm loving it here.'

'That's all well and good,' Patricia interrupted, 'before Betsy comes, quickly tell me how she's doing, and what the situation is with you and that man.'

There was never any fudging things where her mother was concerned. Gill sighed and decided she might as well get it over with. 'Aunt Betsy must tell you herself how she's feeling, but I'd say much better than when I first saw her. As for Luke, he knows all about Michael, and we've got close working together these last few days. He's a lovely man, and I think we might have something good — but don't panic, because we're not about to rush into anything.'

'That's not how it looked when we came in.' Patricia's acerbic observation brought back memories of her fifteen-year-old self being caught snogging her first boyfriend in the front room one Sunday afternoon.

'Leave that poor girl alone, Patty,' Betsy declared as she walked towards them. 'She's a good kid and my Luke is a fine man. Stop bossing them around.'

Patricia turned to face her sister and for a second didn't say anything, clearly studying her closely. 'Oh, Bet, love. What's up with you?'

Then they were in each other's arms, crying and laughing at the same time. Gill caught her father's eye, and he only shrugged as if to say he was staying out of this. Wise man. Luke beckoned to her over their shoulders and she followed him towards the kitchen.

'Tea time, I think,' he joked as he went over to the sink to fill up the kettle and put it on to boil. 'Isn't that the

English cure for everything from flood to famine?'

'Sorry about my mum. She's a bit protective. Especially after . . . Michael,' Gill explained.

'I don't blame her. You're lucky she loves you enough to care.' His gentle admonition touched her heart.

She nodded, unable to imagine the pain that must gnaw at him every day. 'I know.'

'I'll talk to her later. When things are quieter,' he said as he carried on putting a tray together. He sliced pieces of the fresh chocolate cake he'd made that morning at Betsy's request after Gill had stared helplessly at the recipe as if it were written in Chinese. 'Come on, let's get this lot out. Did you have time to get the rooms cleaned earlier?'

'Yes. How about we put my parents in the Helena Suite?' she suggested.

'Sounds good.' He picked up the heavy tray and headed back out to face the fray.

31

'I think it's time for bed,' Patricia declared. She pushed aside her empty plate and fixed her attention back on Gill. 'You can take us up to our room now.'

Luke quickly jumped up. 'I'll bring your bags.' Gill was grateful he wasn't leaving her to face her mother alone.

'Betsy, get yourself some sleep and we'll talk more tomorrow,' Patricia said. 'I want to meet your friend in the morning as well.'

Gill suppressed a smile at the sight of her aunt blushing like a young girl. Her mother had already winkled the story of Thaddeus out, along with more details of Betsy's illness. When her mother heard her sister admit to turning down treatments, she hadn't held back on telling her off. Gill had no doubt she and Luke were next on her mother's hit list.

They all made their way upstairs, and

after the room was examined and declared suitable, Gill almost thought they were going to get away with it, but she should have known better.

'Right. I'm tired, and my dear husband will start nagging in a minute.' Patricia gave Gill's father a wry smile. 'But I won't sleep until I find out more about his man who's apparently wrapped you around his little finger.'

Gill started to protest, but Luke shook his head and squeezed her hand. 'Of course, Mrs Robinson.' He tugged her over with him to the small sofa by the window, and for the next fifteen minutes Gill could only sit in amazement as he patiently related every detail of his life. He held nothing back, and she knew this intensely private man was making a huge leap of faith for her. It took all her self-control not to tell him in front of everyone how much she loved him.

Patricia turned to Gill, her eyes moist with unshed tears. 'I hope you appreciate what a decent man you've found here.'

'Oh, I do,' she replied, too grateful for her mother's realization to throw back at her how dubious she'd been earlier.

Her father suddenly spoke up. 'Right. It's time for me to put my foot down. This lady of mine is supposed not to be overdoing it, so I'm declaring the inquisition over with for today.'

'I was not . . . ' Patricia tried to argue, but Gill's father wasn't having it.

'Off you go, you two.' He fixed a firm stare on them and Luke didn't wait to be asked twice. He hauled Gill towards the door as if the room were on fire and they needed to evacuate the building.

'I didn't even get a chance to say good night,' she protested, but he silenced her with a swift, hard kiss, taking her breath away.

'I assume they'll be staying a while. You'll have other chances,' Luke stated firmly. 'Right now we're going to take some time for ourselves. I cleared it with Betsy earlier, and she and Thaddeus will keep an eye on things while we go on a date.'

'A date?'

'Yes. One of those things people do who want to get to know each other better,' he explained patiently, as if she were a rather slow student. 'We're going out to dinner — one we don't have to cook ourselves.' He led her towards the stairs and they headed down. At the bottom he stopped and gave her a mischievous smile. 'If you'd like to dress up a bit, I won't object. In fact, I might even dig up the suit and tie you drooled over the day we met, if you're very good.'

Gill thought about objecting to his comment but kept her mouth shut. She couldn't imagine where they'd be going around the local area that would demand all this effort, but if he was prepared to take the trouble to change she could do the same.

'The car will be here for us in thirty minutes.' He gave her backside a light tap. 'Off you go, Cinderella.'

Before she could consider asking any

more questions, Gill found herself walking down the hall towards her room with Luke's happy whistles echoing in her ears as he disappeared to get ready.

★　★　★

'Wow, you sure do clean up well.' The humour running through Luke's voice contrasted with his smouldering eyes as his gaze swept down over her.

Gill swallowed hard. He'd reincarnated the smooth, handsome man who'd taken her breath away the first day they'd met, and for a moment her confidence wobbled.

'It's just a suit,' he explained gently. 'If it helps, seeing you in that sexy dress with your hair all fancy has the same effect on me.' He stared at her again. 'Makes me realize you're out of my league.'

'Don't talk rubbish.'

His deep, rumbling laugh filled the room. 'You won't let me be a miserable so-and-so for long, will you?'

'Certainly not,' Gill declared. 'Now, are you taking me out or not?'

He held out his arm and she slid hers in through, loving it when he clasped her hand and pulled her tight. Leading her towards the door, he opened it to let her walk out first. Gill beamed at the sight of the Mockingbird Farm's gleaming Mercedes waiting for them.

'Cinderella, you shall go to the ball,' Luke said teasingly, and ushered her forward.

'Thank you, Prince Charming.' He started to argue, but she tossed him a warning glance and he shut up. Then he helped her in as their driver held the door open, and they settled in the back seat together.

Gill was only sorry it was dark already, so she couldn't truly appreciate the scenery on their way there. Eventually they turned off the main road and headed down a long driveway. As a large building surrounded by other buildings came into view, she gasped. 'It's gorgeous.'

Mockingbird Farm billed itself as a high-class rural resort — a combination of wood cabins with every amenity, champagne and traditional southern cooking. They were going to be dining in the main house, and Gill could hardly wait.

'I used the fact we'd helped them out with the wedding guests to score one of their prized tables overlooking the garden,' Luke explained with a satisfied smile. 'It's floodlit, and there's a spectacular fountain. In we go.' He jumped out of the car and held out his hand.

Gill didn't hesitate.

★ ★ ★

Much later, she pushed her chair away from the table and sighed with happiness. The meal was truly wonderful, and she hadn't been able to resist eating far too much.

'More champagne?' Luke offered, holding up the bottle.

'No, thanks, or you'll be carrying me home,' Gill said with a laugh, and leaned over to kiss his cheek.

'Gill, I . . . ' Luke's brow furrowed as a buzzing noise interrupted the moment. 'Darn it. I'm sorry.' He dragged his phone from his pocket. 'I left it on in case Betsy had any problems.'

'Don't worry, go ahead,' Gill said.

In a matter of seconds, all the colour drained from Luke's face, leaving him grey and drawn. His other hand, resting on the table, started to shake, and Gill placed hers over it in an attempt to remind him that he wasn't alone. He mumbled something she couldn't catch and turned the phone off.

'Is something wrong at the inn?' Gill asked quietly.

He shook his head and cleared his throat before trying to speak. 'That was Harry.' His voice broke.

Gill took a wild guess. 'He's tracked down your mother?'

'Yep.' The word was dragged from his throat, and at that moment Gill wished she'd never set all this in motion.

'How about we get some fresh air and ask to be served coffee outside? It's chilly, but the waiter said there were heaters,' Gill suggested, and Luke managed to nod.

Out on the patio, she rested her head on his shoulder and listened quietly as he told her what Harry had discovered. He'd tracked down Luke's mother, Elena Swinton, through the necklace that her wealthy father had commissioned for her sixteenth birthday. At first she'd denied all knowledge of any baby, but then broke down and admitted the truth.

Elena told Harry how she'd hidden her pregnancy from her family. Being young and skinny, she'd easily disguised her slight weight gain under loose clothes. She'd seen the appeals from the hospital about Luke, but forced herself not to reply for what she thought was his own good. Afterwards she'd thrown herself into work in the family's Napa Valley wine business.

'She never married or had any other children because she thought she didn't deserve to be happy.' Luke's voice shook with emotion. 'She's catching the overnight flight from Los Angeles and arrives in Knoxville at about nine tomorrow morning. She told Harry she'd give anything to meet me, but that it was my choice,' he whispered into Gill's skin. 'After wanting to know who she was for so long, now I'm scared. What do you think?'

'If you don't see her you'll always wonder, but just don't expect too much,' Gill cautioned.

Pain filled his gaze. 'I don't expect anything. I gave up on that a long time ago,' he carried on before she could argue. 'But you're right. I need to do this.' A touch of his usual strength returned and he straightened up, pulling her to him. 'I'm going to ask her to get a taxi to the inn. I can't meet her at the airport. I need you all around me.'

Absurdly pleased, Gill held on tight

and crossed her fingers behind his back. She didn't know if she could bear to see him hurt any worse than he already had been.

32

Gill swallowed hard as Elena Swinton raised her hand to Luke's face, touching his cheek gently as if he might disappear again.

'My baby boy,' she murmured, seemingly unaware of the tears streaming down her face. 'I never forgot you. Not for a single day. When it was cold and raining I wondered if you were somewhere warm and dry. Every time I sat down to eat, I worried you were starving somewhere.'

Luke took a step closer, and Gill held her breath. 'Please don't torture yourself any more,' he said. 'I understand now that you did the best you could for me, even if I didn't always see it that way. I had a few troubles growing up, but I'm good these days, and I've got lots of people who love and care for me.' He explained everything so tenderly, it about broke Gill's heart all over again, and she could only guess the effect it was having on his mother.

Luke put his arm around Elena's shoulders and started to introduce her to them all. When he reached Gill, a loving expression lit up his face. 'This is Gill Robinson. She's Betsy's niece and came over to help us over the holidays. I . . . care for her very much, and I hope she's going to be a large part of my life.'

'I'm sure she's very special,' Elena said with a sly smile that so resembled Luke's it took Gill's breath away for a moment.

Soon they were all settled down on the sofas around the Christmas tree, drinking coffee and swapping stories. Luke caught Gill's eye and gestured towards the kitchen. 'Would you excuse us a moment? We're going to organize some lunch,' he said, and grabbed her hand to take her along with him.

'For a woman who hates cooking, how do I always end up in the kitchen?' Gill teased as soon as the door closed behind them. Luke swiftly pulled her into his arms and kissed her, taking his time and making her melt.

'Because it's the only place I can ever get you on your own,' he declared with a broad smile. 'I'm sure we'll only have a few minutes before someone decides to offer their help, so I'll be quick. I don't intend to rush you into anything, no matter how badly I want to.' A tinge of heat coloured his cheeks and Gill blushed along with him. 'How about I simply tell you that this has been my best Christmas ever and I can't wait for the New Year?'

'That works, and I totally agree. Now stop talking and kiss me,' Gill replied with a giggle. 'After that, it's time to get another meal ready, I suppose.' She was pretending to complain, but Luke took no notice. He followed her orders and proceeded to make her Christmas complete.